Decoy

Club Confession Series, Volume 3

Lexy Timms

Published by Dark Shadow Publishing, 2022.

This is a work of fiction. Similarities to real people, places, or events are entirely coincidental.

DECOY

First edition. May 4, 2022.

Copyright © 2022 Lexy Timms.

Written by Lexy Timms.

CLUB CONFESSION #3
decoy
USA TODAY BESTSELLING AUTHOR
LEXY TIMMS

1.	http://bookcoverbydesign.co.uk/

Club Confession Series

Envy

Crave

Decoy

Urge

Path

Find Lexy Timms:

Lexy Timms Newsletter:
http://www.lexytimms.com/newsletter
Lexy Timms Facebook Page:
https://www.facebook.com/LexyTimmsAuthor
Lexy Timms Website:
http://www.lexytimms.com

Want to read more...
For **FREE?**
Sign up for Lexy Timms' newsletter
And she'll send you updates on new releases, ARC copies of books
and a whole lotta fun!
Sign up for news and updates!
http://www.lexytimms.com/newsletter

Decoy

SILENCE IS A DECOY of the coming storm...

If there's one thing I know for sure - it's that I'm not going to let Nadia go without a fight.

The woman I love is halfway across the world from me, fleeing the city with her father to try and keep her family safe - but the man she's turned to for help will do far more harm than good. I need to get her out, but with the authorities breathing down my neck, I don't know how I can.

When the one person I can trust in New York comes under threat, I'm forced out on my own. The only thing between Nadia and the monster who wants her is me - and I will go to any lengths to get her back.

CLUB CONFESSION
deco
USA TODAY BESTSELLING AUTHOR
LEXY TIMM
CLUB CONFESSION #2
decoy
USA TODAY BESTSELLING AUTHOR
LEXY TIMMS
GET IT ON
Google Play
kobo
Available at
amazon
nook
Lexy Timms

Chapter One

Nadia

As soon as I saw Mauro, I tried to turn my back and get the hell out of there.

What the fuck was he doing here? My mind raced as I tried to make sense of it, any kind of sense of it, but nothing was clear. It felt too convoluted to figure out, even though I knew I was going to need to.

But I crashed straight into a couple of stern-looking men about twice my size, and I knew I wasn't going to be able to get out of this so easily. My heart thudded heavy against my chest – what was happening? Why was Mauro here? Didn't he know that I was in the middle of something pretty damn important right now?

They marched me back over to Mauro, who watched me with a grim expression on his face. My heart wouldn't slow as I tried to steady myself. I had no idea what to expect with all of this, but I wasn't going to show him even an inch of fear right now. I had been through too much for that. Nothing was going to stop me.

"What do you want?" I asked him, voice as curt as I could make it. He sighed, and suddenly, it was like he had aged thirty years at once.

"I want you to leave. But there's something I need you to know before you do."

I tensed up. I didn't like the sound of this, didn't like where this was going. Hadn't I been through enough already? Hadn't I dragged my ass through this nightmare for too long as it was? What else could there be for me to find out? I had never asked to be part of this world. I had just had it thrust upon me out of nowhere, and now that I was so close to getting out, here Mauro was, trying to stop me from making a clean break.

"What is it?" I snapped, crossing my arms over my chest and glancing reproachfully up at the guards on either side of me. I didn't need to be manhandled around this airport like I was going to make a break for it. I was so close to getting out, and nothing was going to keep me here in New York, not if I could help it.

"I've been working with the Serbians this entire time," Mauro admitted to me, and his voice dropped, as though he could hardly believe that he was saying it out loud. I stared at him.

"What do you mean?"

"Ever since Andreas' father died," he continued. "I knew that – well, I knew that Andreas was hot-headed, and I knew he might not be able to handle the weight of it all on his head when he first came to power. So... I stepped in. I helped. I needed to make sure that he wouldn't land himself in more trouble than he could handle, so I did what I thought I had to."

I shook my head. Did Andreas have any idea about this? I would bet not – if he'd found out his right-hand man had been working with the Serbs, it would have wrecked him.

"It was the only way to keep the peace," he went on, defensive. "I'd do it again. I did what needed to be done, you have to understand that."

"I don't know why you're trying to convince me," I muttered. I wasn't the one he had betrayed – that was Andreas, and he knew it.

"They've got the city," he told me, his voice cracking. "I – it's not the way I wanted it to go down, trust me. If I could have done anything to make sure that Andreas and his father's legacy stayed where they were meant to be, I would have, but it's too late for that now."

"What do you mean, too late?" I demanded. Had something happened to Andreas? Was he hurt? Why was Mauro so sure that this was the end?

"I can't get into all of that now," he replied, shaking his head. "But it's over. The Serbs rule in this city, it's done."

"Is Andreas safe—"

"I can't talk to you about that," he told me, bluntly. He was hardly letting me get a word out. I wondered if this was actually about him telling me the truth, or just getting whatever was bothering him off of his chest before I left for good. I was a confession booth to him right now, a chance to get this out of his head before he had to tell the truth to Andreas, and I hated that.

"Then why are you talking to me at all?" I demanded. He knew I cared about Andreas above all of this – even in the chaos that Nikita had dragged into our lives, I still thought of Andreas first and foremost, needed him to be okay.

"I'm the one who arranged for you to get out of the city," he explained. "I'm the one who's getting you and your father to Serbia. And I need to know that you're going to go through with it."

"What about the fact that I came all the way down here makes you think that I wouldn't?" I demanded, shaking my head. "Do you hear yourself?"

"Andreas is going to do everything he can to try and stop you," he admitted. "He's going to do what he can to try and get you back, but he has no idea how to handle all of this. He doesn't know what he's up against, and all he cares about..."

He eyed me, for a long moment, inhaling deeply as he tried to get a handle on all of this.

"All he cares about is you, and I'm not sure there's much I can do to change that. He'll do whatever he can to keep you close to him, but I need to know that you and your father are gone. And that you're not coming back."

"If Andreas wants me here, then that's our decision to make."

"I can't talk you out of it," he agreed. "But I – I can tell you for sure that you need to think long and hard about who's going to be able to protect you and your father if you choose to stay in the city. Now that the Serbs are taking over, you can't rely on the Italians to keep you safe. And if something happens to you..."

He trailed off, leaving the threat of it hanging in the air menacingly. I knew what he was trying to tell me. He wasn't going to come out and say that my father and I were dead meat, but he didn't have to – I could already tell that was what he meant, and I didn't much feel like fighting him on it.

I felt something clam shut inside of me, something tightening in a way I couldn't escape from. I was locked in now, I had no choice but to run, and the thought of that scared the shit out of me. I had no idea how I was going to make it out of this in one piece, but I had to find a way to try.

"So what do you want me to do with that?" I demanded. "Where do I go from here?"

Mauro's eyes darted this way and that, making sure that nobody was listening to us.

"I'm asking you to get on that plane and tell Nikita anything that he needs to hear from you," he replied. "And get out of this city. Stay out of it. What's going to come next, you don't want to be here for it."

I chewed on my lip. I wasn't sure if I trusted him, but then, who else knew the extent of everything that was happening here? He was the person who had the most control over all of this, the one who could twist the screws to make things fit the way he wanted. I had no choice but to trust him right now. This wasn't just about me, it was about my father, too, and he was relying on me to make the choice that would allow both of us to get out of here alive.

"Will I ever get to see Andreas again? If I get on that plane?" I asked him bluntly. That was the question that was caught in the web of my mind right now, the one I couldn't let go. I couldn't imagine being without him, but at the same time – if I had to run, for the sake of my family, I knew it was what he would have wanted for me.

"I don't know," Mauro admitted. "But I do know for sure that it's not safe for the two of you to be around each other right now, do you understand? If you don't leave, he's going to be distracted trying to look out for you, and if that happens..."

He shook his head ominously. I knew what was on the line here, we both did, knew that the stakes were dangerously high. I just didn't want to admit that I had no choice but to leave him behind; it didn't feel right, not after all that we had been through. I wished I could just see him again, one more time, tell him that this wasn't my choice and that I would have stayed if I could have...

"I get it," I replied, finally.

"There might be some point, far down the line, where the two of you can see each other again," he offered me. "Far from this place, of course. But I don't know when that might be. Or if it'll even happen."

I nodded. At least he was being honest with me. That was the most I could ask for right now, now that I was running – now that I had no choice but to put as much distance between myself and the man that I loved as I could.

"You need to go, Nadia," he urged me. "I can't tell you any more. Just... leave. And don't let anything Andreas says convince you that you should come back."

"I will," I promised him, even though the words seemed to choke in my throat as I tried to get them out. How could I do this to him? I was sure he would never forgive me, or at least that he would put up a fight to keep me close – he hadn't let me just walk out of his life to Miami, after all, and I was certain that he would do what he could to pull me back to the city once he knew I was gone.

But I had to stand strong. I had no idea what the future was going to bring, but I had to trust that Mauro knew what he was talking about when he told me to get out. It was the best thing for my father and I, even though I didn't exactly want to put any trust at all in Nikita – I didn't believe he was the best person to protect us, but he was about the only option we had right now, so I didn't have much of a choice.

The bodyguards stepped aside to let me go, and I started back towards the plane. My heart was thrumming in my chest, but I tried to ignore it. I was making the right choice, even if it didn't feel like the easiest one – I was making the choice that I needed to make, the one my survival hinged on.

And so, I did my very best to ignore the tears dripping down my face as I went to leave this city – and Andreas – for good.

Chapter Two

Andreas

I PACED BACK AND FORTH in my apartment, trying to burn off the energy that was coursing through my system. I felt as though I was going to blow a vein at any moment, but I couldn't get out of here, couldn't run to see what was happening in the rest of the city – I had to obey Mauro, and stay put.

He had told me, in no uncertain terms, that I was to remain right here while he tried to work out what was going on throughout the city, and especially with Kozlov. He was sure there was something up, and he was going to make sure he didn't let anything happen to me as a result.

"You have to trust me," he told me, as he pulled on his coat. "Stay here. I'll check what's happening on the streets, and I'll get back to you."

"You could get hurt—"

"Not as much as you could," he replied, shaking his head. "You need to stay here. It's the only way we can be sure you keep safe."

I sighed. I wasn't sure I believed him. How could I be sure I'd stay safe anywhere in this city, now that the Serbs seemed to have run out of patience waiting for me to make a choice? I needed to know what the hell was going on, and there was only one way I could do that – send Mauro out, let him get the feel of the city, find out what was going on out there.

I wished I could talk to Nadia, but I knew she was the last person I should be thinking of in that moment. Shit, I couldn't believe she had really turned her back on me when I had been doing everything I could to help her. It just didn't make any sense. She must have seen how sick it was, that she would leave after all we had been through, but maybe I had misread everything that had happened between us. Maybe I had seen more depth to our relationship than there ever had been. Maybe I had wanted it to be there, because I had put so much on the line to try and make sure that she was okay, and then...

I didn't even have the end to that sentence yet. I had no idea what she had done. She could have run, sure, she could have put as much distance between me and her as she could, or maybe she was just putting on an act so she could come back to me once the heat was off. That was what I was clinging to with all my might, the belief that she might return when all of this was over.

Though, the more time passed, the more and more clear it seemed to become that she was just... gone. And that I was going to have to get used to it. I never thought that she could pull something like that, but honestly, maybe I needed to switch up my expectations of her, of everyone else around me.

It was far too easy for me to believe that people meant better than they did. Especially when it came to Nadia – Hell, from the moment I'd seen her, it had been like everything else had just vanished from my mind, all the focus I'd had on my father's empire was gone, just like that. I couldn't fight it, didn't want to – I just knew I wanted her, and I would have done anything at all to make sure I had her.

And look where it had gotten me. I didn't even know if she was safe, and that was enough to make me fucking sick – even if she wasn't anywhere close to me, or New York, I wanted to know she had nothing to worry about. I wished I could have sent some of my men out after her, but I was sure Nikita would have clocked on and worked out that I was trying to track her down. And I doubted he would have taken too kindly to that.

And so, there I was, stuck in my apartment, unable to do anything but wait for some new information as I prayed Nadia and her father had made it out of the city okay. I couldn't believe I was pulling for them to have left, but what choice did I have? If they had stayed, they would have been in even more danger, and I didn't want that for her, for either of them. Nadia wasn't part of this world, or at least, she hadn't been until I had pulled her into it. It was only fair that she get out of it in one piece, never have to look back and see what she had left behind.

Would she miss me? I wished I could ask her that much. There was so much I wanted to say to her, even now – so much I wished I could have spoken out loud, before she was out of my life for good. That I loved her, that I was grateful she had been part of my life, that she had shown me there was more to me than I had ever thought. That I believed I could fall in love now, in a way I never had before, and that I had her to thank for that. I prayed she knew all of that already, I would never have been able to forgive myself if she had gone out there thinking I didn't care for her...

But there was nothing I could do about that now. I had to hold steady and wait for information from Mauro, hope he was getting me what I needed. Pray the Serbs hadn't done anything to hurt him. I hated not being able to push this forward myself, but Mauro was right, I needed to hide out and make sure I didn't attract any more attention than I already had. Shit was already chaos right now, the last thing I needed was a bullet in my gut to turn it up to eleven on the bullshit scale.

I was going to pour myself a drink when my phone buzzed, and I snatched it up at once. I didn't recognize the number, but that wasn't exactly new – burner phones were a fact of life in this business, and I knew that whoever was on the other end just didn't want me to know who they were. I answered it immediately.

"Hello?"

"Andreas?"

The voice that came down the line was muffled, as though whoever it belonged to was doing their best to disguise it; I frowned, trying to pick out more information about them through the strange front they were putting on.

"Yes?"

"You have enemies who are posing as friends," the voice continued. Whoever it was, I was certain that they didn't want me to hear their actual voice, and that bugged me – who the fuck was calling me with no intention of actually letting me hear what they had to say?

"Who?" I demanded.

"Not Nadia or her father."

My spine prickled when I heard them say her name. I didn't like that she seemed to have become a part of this. It wasn't what she deserved, and I knew she was safer if fewer people knew about her.

The accent, that was what I was having a hard time placing – I couldn't work out if it belonged to someone I knew or not. It sounded vaguely familiar, but that could have been because it was Eastern European – maybe Serbian? I'd heard enough of those the last few weeks to burn the memory of them into my head, and I couldn't work out who with that kind of voice would have been willing to talk to me.

"How do you know that name?" I demanded. I couldn't make sense of any of this, but I supposed that was the point – whoever it was on the other end of the line wanted me to have to dissect every word they said, and I needed to take it all in before they decided they were done with me.

"Look at the people closest to you," the voice continued. "That's all I can say."

And with that, the line went dead, leaving me even more confused than I had been at the beginning of the call.

What the fuck were they talking about? Enemies posing as friends? What did that mean? Whoever it was seemed intent on making sure that I didn't mistake Nadia as one of those people, but that didn't clear up much in my head. What were they talking about? Who were they talking about? Was this just an attempt to get me even more confused than I had been before? They must have known that I was starved for information, that I would take anything I could get, but this – this was a lot more oblique than I had been prepared for.

I poured myself a bourbon and took a long sip. It was going to be one hell of a night, I could tell that much, and random phone calls from people on burners who didn't even seem to want to use their real voices weren't going to help with that. Mauro would have told me to get some sleep, but I knew there was no way that I would have managed. I'd just toss and turn, thinking of her, of Nadia, of how much I wanted to make sure that she was okay, and that would have been useless.

The people closest to me. There weren't many of those – I considered the few I had as I turned those words over in my head. Maybe someone who worked for me at one of the clubs? Or maybe—

Before I could think on it any longer, my phone rang again, and this time, Mauro was the one calling me. I answered at once.

"What's going on?" I demanded. I had been waiting long enough, and I had no idea where he had gone, what exactly he had been up to all this time. I needed to know what was going on, even if it wasn't what I wanted to hear.

"I haven't been able to get hold of Nadia yet," he explained, and he sounded almost out of breath, as though he had been sprinting right before he had put in this call. What was going on? Was he all right?

"Are you okay—"

"I'm fine," he replied quickly, a little too quickly, as though he wanted to shut down any doubts I might have had before they could take root in my mind. He knew I could get way too far into paranoia if I wasn't careful, and that would only lead to chaos in the state that I was in right now. I needed to hold myself together, no matter how hard it might be. I felt like an animal locked up in a zoo, but I wouldn't stay like this for long – as soon as I found out what was happening with Nadia, I would be able to relax a little.

"Do you have eyes on her?" I pressed. I had no idea how he could, given that we hadn't known she was going to make a break for it until it was too late, but I desperately hoped he would say yes.

"I don't have much, but the guys I do have last spotted her getting off a plane in St. Petersburg," he explained. "They think she's going to carry on to Serbia. I wouldn't be surprised if she passes straight through and we lose her after that."

"What guys do you have down there?" I asked, confused. All the way in Serbia? It wasn't like we had any connections down there, any reason for him to bother with a place like that. What was the point of him having contacts all the way out there?

"Just old friends," he replied quickly. A little too quickly. I frowned. "Do I know them?"

"No, they were – I worked with them before I met your father."

"Can we trust them?" I asked. I didn't want to tell him about the phone call I had received yet, no need to worry him with something as heavy as that, but I needed to know he wasn't putting too much of our information on the line.

"Of course we can," Mauro shot back, and he sounded a little annoyed that I was even questioning him on that. But come on – did he really expect me to just let him tell anyone what was happening right now? This was serious. We were in the midst of something huge, something bigger than anything we had dealt with before, and there was no way that I was going to allow him to brush me off as though I was crazy for wanting more.

"Then tell me who they are," I replied, trying to keep my voice steady. He paused, hesitated – and I felt a rush of panic hit me. Why couldn't he just tell me? What the fuck was going on right now?

"I'll explain it all once I'm back at your place," he promised. "It's hard to get into over the phone. I'll speak to you soon, okay?"

And with that, he hung up before I could say another word. I didn't like this – didn't like it one fucking bit. But I knew that Mauro wasn't going to let me choose how all of this went. He had his contacts, he had a life before my father and I.

And right now, I didn't like that one little bit. I needed to know everything that was happening, everyone who was involved, and the way he was dancing around answering my questions didn't sit right to me. I needed to get him to tell me what was happening, but I had no clue how I was meant to do that, not really. If Mauro had secrets, it was going to take a hell of a lot for me to get them out of him.

But maybe I needed to push a little harder to make sure that I did. Because I couldn't risk having anyone keeping shit from me right now – least of all the one person I was meant to be able to trust above everyone else.

Chapter Three

Nadia

AS I HEADED UP THE steps to the plane, my feet dragged underneath me in protest. I didn't want to do this, didn't want to actually leave the city, but I didn't have a choice right now. I had to get out, and I had to make sure I didn't wind up making more of a mess of this than I already had.

I hated myself more than I could put into words right now. How had I managed to screw up my life this badly? I needed to go back, to tell Andreas I wanted to be with him and that I couldn't leave without him, but I knew that staying would have been the wrong choice. Mauro had made that much clear – whatever was happening, Andreas didn't have control of it any longer, and the best I could do was pray that he didn't get hurt. Or worse.

The private jet that was waiting for me was gorgeously well-appointed, and any other time I would have been excited to take a trip in a plane as fancy as this. But right now, I wished I could reel back time and leave the airport before I had even arrived. Life before all of this hadn't exactly been easy, but at least it had somewhat felt like it had been in my control. This, now? It was utterly beyond my realm of comprehension, everything rushing around me so fast that I hardly had time to take it all in. I wanted to leave it all behind, but I couldn't; this life would always follow me, the memories of what I'd had before I had fallen for the wrong man and managed to blow it all up in my own face.

Nikita was waiting for me in the plane, and he greeted me with a warm hug; I was stiff in his arms, not wanting him to think for a moment that I appreciated the gesture. I hated being close to him. Hated having to rely on him. He must have known that, but I got the feeling that there was some part of him that enjoyed it – some part of him that loved knowing I had no choice but to hand myself over to him.

"You made the right choice coming here, Nadia," he told me, squeezing my hand. He was acting sweet now, but I was sure there was something darker beneath the surface, something he was doing his best to cover up and pretend wasn't there at all. I wished that I could call it out, but that was far too dangerous. I needed to go along with this for the time being, at least until I got out of this plane and as far from him as possible.

"Here, take a seat, you must be exhausted," he continued, guiding me to a plush leather chair stacked with pillows; I sank down on to the edge of it, staring out the window, not wanting to make eye contact with him. He was wearing heavy aftershave, and it felt like it was sliding down my throat and choking me. Surely, he had better things to do than hover over me this entire time? I almost wanted to point that out to him, but I knew that it wouldn't get me anywhere. I had to play by his rules now, and hope for the best – hope it would be enough to get me out of this mess in one piece.

"There, isn't that better?" he told me. I nodded.

"Thanks."

"I'm so glad you're here with us, Nadia," he continued, voice smooth, his words picked carefully. This was a man who was used to getting what he wanted, and had no issue at all talking around the people close to him to make sure that happened.

"Are you comfortable?" he asked. I didn't reply. I couldn't lie like that to him. I knew that he would never have bought it, anyway.

"You know, Nadia, I'm not a bad guy," he told me, leaning forward, clearly trying to get me to look at him. I couldn't. It wasn't even out of stubbornness, I just didn't think I could turn to face him without feeling a wave of nausea at what I had just done – coming here, running to him for help. He knew that he had me right where he wanted me, and I resented that on a level that I couldn't even really put into words. I didn't want to have to rely on anyone, let alone this fucking creep, but he wasn't giving me much of a choice.

"And I'll prove that to you," he continued. "As soon as you give me the chance. Trust me, you made the right decision, coming here with us instead of sticking it out with Andreas…"

It let that last word hang in the air for a long moment, seeming to notice how I tensed when he said it. I couldn't even think about Andreas right now, not without feeling that deep, grinding loss – not without being reminded of how far I was from him, how distant we were. It was only going to get worse, I was only going to get further from him, and I had no idea how I was going to survive all that distance between us.

"He's a playboy, Nadia, and he would have hurt you the same way that he hurt almost every woman who was unlucky enough to come into his life," he went on, smoothly. "Did he ever tell you about the girls he was with before?"

I shook my head. I hadn't asked much about his previous dating life. I hadn't wanted to. I figured it was something he would share with me when he wanted to, if he ever did. I knew that Nikita could just be spinning bullshit to me, but something nagged at the back of my mind, warning me that it was true.

"Yes, that's what I thought," Nikita agreed. "He wouldn't want you to know about all the hurt he'd done to them – that makes sense."

I looked out of the window. I didn't want to give Nikita an inch, I knew he would take a mile. But a part of me was curious to find out what was going on with Andreas, if there really had been girls before me – and, if so, what the hell had happened to them.

"Trust me when I say that it wouldn't have ended well for you two," he remarked. "Especially you, Nadia. It never does, not for the women in his life. You're safer coming with me than staying here with him to get your heart broken – or worse."

I couldn't reply. I didn't know what he expected me to say right now. I wasn't going to just quietly agree with him, though I could tell that was what he hoped for – he hoped he had managed to beat me down enough that I would go along with anything he said to me, but I wasn't there, not yet. I knew Andreas had more to him than Nikita wanted me to believe, and I wasn't going to write off everything that had happened between us, just because Nikita seemed certain that he knew him better than I did.

"You need someone who really wants to take care of you," he continued, leaning a little closer to me. I locked eyes with him finally, and that dark, shark-like gaze of his made the hairs on the back of my neck stand up. I wanted to shove him away, but I knew I had to play along, at least for now. Knew that I had to give him what he wanted.

"Someone who's a little more... mature," he went on, smiling a little wider. "Someone who wants the best for you."

He let those words hang in the air for a while, and I could tell he was doing his very best to coax a response out of me, but I chose not to give it to him. I yawned, covering my mouth and hoping he would take that as the chance to excuse himself that it was.

"I'll leave you to get some rest," he murmured, patting my arm again. I hated it when he touched me – whenever he laid his hands on me, it was as though he was trying his best to make sure I knew I belonged to him now. I had made my choice, and that meant I was completely at his mercy. Nikita was a dangerous man, I knew that much for sure, and I had no idea how long I would last with him hanging over my shoulder, trying to get under my skin, trying to make it so I didn't have anything else to fall back on.

"Would you like something to drink?" he pressed, clearly trying to get some sort of reaction out of me.

"No, thank you," I replied, making sure I didn't give away anything in my tone of voice. There was no way I was going to let him read into what was happening here – as far as I was concerned, I was going to have nothing to do with this man, I just needed to get out of New York and he was the quickest way to make that happen.

He eyed me for a moment longer, clearly waiting for me to say something else. Maybe he expected me to throw myself at his feet or something, tell him how grateful I was for everything he had done for me? But I wasn't going to let him think he had that much control over me. I was in charge here. At least, for now. In this conversation, if nothing else.

"Well, I'll leave you to it," he remarked, voice arched with annoyance at my lack of response to the way he was speaking to me. I ignored it. I wasn't going to let him get under my skin. He rose to his feet and backed away from my chair, much to my relief, and left me to my own thoughts for a while.

Shit, I had no idea what I was going to do next. No idea how I was going to get out of all of this in one piece. It just... it felt like far too much for me to handle, the possibility of everything that might come once this plane had landed. Even if Nikita backed off for good, I had a whole new life to make for myself, and I didn't have a clue what that was going to look like, not really. How could I just start over like this? How was I meant to forget everything that I'd had back in New York? It didn't seem possible, not even close, and I had no idea how I was supposed to get through all of this without losing my mind.

Plus, the way Nikita was talking... it was clear he wanted me single. He wanted me ready for him, if he chose to make that move. I had no idea how I was going to shut that down without pissing him off, but I was going to have to try. I couldn't stand the thought of him looking at me in that way, but I knew he wasn't a guy you said no to, not if you could avoid it, and he was going to do everything he could to push me into a corner where I felt like I didn't have any choice but to go along with everything he was pushing on me.

I tucked my legs up to my chest and wrapped my arms around them. I just wanted to vanish into myself, more than anything – wanted to forget that I was here, that I was in this mess, that this was happening to me at all.

But I was here, and nothing was going to change that, no matter how hard I wished for it. I just had to keep pushing forward, and hope my father and I would come out the other side of this alive.

And that, one day, I might get a chance to explain to Andreas why I had fled from him the way I had.

Chapter Four

Andreas

ARRIVING AT THE CLUB, I tried to ignore the nagging discomfort at the back of my mind. Something was up, I was sure of it – but I had no idea what, or whether it was just my own paranoid overthinking that had me convinced.

Mauro had insisted I come down to this meeting just to get out of the apartment for a little while, and honestly, I couldn't say I blamed him. I must have been driving him downright crazy with all the questions that I had, all the demands I needed answered, the ones he didn't seem to have responses for yet. I wished I could have pulled more out of him, but he was being evasive – probably just to protect me, but still...

I was down here to try and secure the deal with the Serbs on the club in their territory, Yosemite's, and I was praying that this just ran as smoothly as it could. I had to make a good impression, prove to everyone here that I could handle anything they threw at me. I knew this might be a make-or-break for the shit that had been bubbling between Kozlov and I all this time.

I couldn't stop thinking about Nadia. How the fuck was I meant to just forget about her? After everything we had been through, it felt ridiculous to believe for an instant that I could. I missed her like crazy, wanted nothing more than for her to be back here, in my arms, where she belonged, but she could have been anywhere on the planet right now and I wouldn't have known a thing about it. Mauro's people hadn't been able to keep too close an eye on her. Or, at least, if they could, he wasn't giving me anything more to work with than I already had.

Maybe because he knew that was the only way to keep my head in the game when it came to everything that was happening here.

If I could have gone to her right then and there, I would have. I would have in an instant. How could anything here in New York matter when the two of us were so far apart? I just wanted to hold her, pull her into my arms again and tell her everything was going to be okay and mean it, but I couldn't - not yet, at least.

Yosemite's was already buzzing with people as I pushed through the crowds, heading towards the manager's office. I had a couple of guards outside and a driver parked around the back in case I needed to make a quick getaway. I hoped Kozlov wouldn't be stupid enough to turn this into something that it didn't have to be, but I didn't trust him as far as I could throw him, and there was no way I was going to take that risk.

In the back, the manager, Grigori, was already waiting for me; his eyes darted back and forth as I stepped inside, checking to see if anyone was with me, if I was armed.

"Good evening," I greeted him. "Thank you for meeting with me tonight."

"Of course, of course," he replied, sounding distracted. What was on his mind? Maybe he was just worried about what might become of him if Nikita found out that he was meeting with me. Surely, he was already aware – he didn't strike me as the kind of man who let much slide past him, and this was a particular sore point for him.

"Please, sit down," he continued, gesturing to the seat on the other side of his desk. My security had advised that I stay standing, in case I needed to make a quick break.

"I'm fine like this," I replied. A bead of sweat dribbled down from his brow to his eye, and he wiped it away quickly. He looked genuinely scared right now.

"You have nothing to worry about from me," I told him, crossing my arms across my chest. "Do I have something to worry about from you, Grigori?"

His face paled, as though I had just said the magic words that exposed him. I felt the bottom of my stomach drop out as he looked up at me, face cringed into a pseudo-apologetic grimace.

"I'm sorry," he whispered. And then, a moment later, the sound of a muffled gunshot cut through the air around us.

I dropped to the ground at once, crawling for the door. I shoved it open, looking out to see where the attack had come from, but nobody in the club seemed to have heard a thing. Shit! I had to get to the back entrance as fast as I could, where my driver was waiting, and lose myself in the crowd in the meantime.

I dove out, got to my feet, and buried myself amongst the throngs of people, hoping that they wouldn't be stupid enough to kill someone who had just come here to have a good time. The reputation of the club would be in tatters – but I didn't know if that mattered to them more than getting rid of me or not, and I didn't want to find out.

I pushed my way through the crowds to the back door, keeping my head low, listening for the familiar sound of a bullet cutting through the people around me – but there was nothing. Either they had lost me, or they weren't risking casualties.

I stumbled to the fire exit at the back, where my driver was waiting for me, and the moment I stepped out, my security team leapt into action.

"Into the car, now!" one of them barked, grabbing me and pushing my head down as another hail of bullets rained from the buildings above us. I was shoved into the back of the car, and he slapped the roof, indicating to the driver to get the hell out of there while I still had a chance of keeping my head.

The car sped away to the street beyond, and I peered behind us, trying to make out if anyone had followed us out of there. No way would the Serbs have risked me making a break for it like this with no recourse – I was sure they would have someone on my tail in no time.

I reached into the compartment in front of me, where the security team kept their weapons, and I grabbed a gun. I knew that I might have to fight, and I needed to be ready to do just that if that's what it came to. It wasn't ideal, but as long as I survived, I would count it as a win.

"There's a car following us," My driver called to me, nodding to the rearview mirror. "Black merc, looks like it's been following since the club—"

He hardly got another word out before a bullet dented the back windshield of the vehicle.

"Shit!" I exclaimed, and I ducked down again, heart hammering. I checked that the gun was loaded, and rolled down the window – I needed to stop them coming after us. I had no idea how long they would follow us, or what it would take to get them to stop, but I was done taking risks.

I leaned out of the window and levelled the gun at the car behind us – I wasn't the greatest marksman in the world, but I just needed to get off some warning shots to scare them off. I fired, three times, glad that we were far enough to the edge of the city that there weren't people crowding the streets to see this.

A bullet whistled past my face and I ducked back into the car, regaining my composure. Shit. I had no idea how many people they had sent after me, but I was certain that they weren't going to be giving up anytime soon. I needed to put up a fight – make it as hard as I could for them to take me, even though they clearly thought they had me right where they wanted me.

I took a breath and leaned out of the car again, this time getting off a shot that hit one of the tires of the pursuing vehicle – I heard the pop, and then watched as it careered off the road and onto the sidewalk.

"Go, go!" I yelled to my driver. This might be the only chance we had to make a break for it. He slammed his foot down and tore off down the street, and I peered out of the back of the car to make sure we were leaving the people who had been after us behind.

The adrenaline was pumping so hard in my veins that I couldn't think straight. How could I have been stupid enough to think I would be able to get away with this? Going to the Serbs' territory, after everything that had happened, I had been asking for trouble, and I knew I was lucky to have gotten out of there in one piece.

We pulled up outside my apartment building, where a half-dozen security guys were already swarming – they must have been tipped off that there had been an attack. I heaved myself out of the car, and one of them helped me to the elevator so that I could get myself to safety. My legs were shaking, the sheer shock and panic of it all coursing through me so fast that I couldn't make sense of it. I wanted to run – I wanted to get out of here, get as far from here as possible, but I needed to hold my ground and prove that they hadn't managed to get rid of me quite yet.

"Stay in there," the security guard told me as he pushed me into the elevator. "In your apartment. We'll keep watch tonight – nobody's going to get close to you."

I nodded, and slumped back against the wall as the elevator doors slid shut in front of me. I closed my eyes, tipped my head back, and tried to gather myself. All of this was so fucking crazy, I could hardly wrap my head around it, but I knew I was going to have to if I was going to survive this mess.

I staggered to my bed and crashed head-first into the covers as soon as I got the chance. Now that the adrenaline was starting to wear off, I was coming back into my body.

And I could feel a grinding pain at my side, something burning with agony that I had been able to ignore up until now. My body had been in fight-or-flight, so intense that I hadn't been able to think about anything else at all.

But now, as I flipped over on the bed and peeled back my shirt to see what was going on, I spotted it. The bloom of blood in the fabric.

And, below that, the mark – the mark where a bullet had entered my skin.

I had been shot.

Chapter Five

Nadia

"HERE WE GO," NIKITA told me, an arm draped around my shoulders as he steered me into the safehouse. I wanted to shrug him off, but I was far too exhausted to think about putting up a fight right now. I just wanted him gone, and I didn't know what it was going to take to convince him that I didn't need him here with me.

"You'll be safe here," he assured me, as though I needed it. The only reason that I was with him was because I knew he would be able to look after me, and honestly, I was starting to wonder if it was actually worth it. The way he had been talking to me, looking at me all this time, I wanted to claw off my skin – it made me sick to see him acting that way, as though he had any business treating me like I was his.

"Thank you," I muttered. I still had to be pleasant to him. I had to make sure I kept him placated, even if that meant swallowing down some of the anger that was coursing through my system in that moment. I hated having to give him any kindness, especially with the way he had been treating me, but it was better to keep him on our side for now and deal with the consequences later.

We had touched down wherever we were about an hour ago, and a car had been waiting for us as soon as we stepped off the aircraft; Nikita had assured me that we would be going to see my father, and honestly, I was so looking forward to laying eyes on him again. I needed to know he was okay. He was the reason I had done this in the first place, and there was no way I was going to be able to follow through if something had happened to him.

The safehouse that we had been brought to wasn't much to look at from the outside, but inside, it was all right – not much in the way of electronics, apart from a stove and a few lights, but I supposed that was their way of making sure nobody found out that we were here. Fine. If that's what it took, I would go along with it for now. I just wanted to see my father.

"Your dad is in the first room on the left, up the stairs," Nikita told me, as though aware that there was only one thing on my mind right now. I hurried up the stairs towards him, my heart beating hard in my chest – I just needed to be sure that he was okay. I needed to see him again, and tell him I had made the call I needed to in order to ensure that we were both safe here.

Sure enough, behind the door that Nikita had pointed me towards, there he was. He was asleep, and I didn't want to wake him, but I slipped into the darkened room and knelt down beside his bed.

"Hey, Dad," I murmured softly. "I – I'm here."

He didn't stir. He was out for the count – that had to be a good thing, right? He was probably exhausted after everything that had happened, and I was pleased to see that he seemed to be getting some rest.

"I'm here," I continued. "I – I'm not going anywhere. If you need me..."

I trailed off. I felt ridiculous, talking to him like this, but I needed to speak with someone right now – someone who I could trust. With Andreas so far from me, I didn't have any other choice but to rely on my father. I hoped he would wake up soon, so I could talk to him, tell him how glad I was that he was here with me. That we were safe, and he had nothing left to worry about anymore, not if I could help it.

I squeezed his hand lightly, and he let out a small grunt and shuffled in his spot. Okay, so he was still alive, that was something – that was why I had come here in the first place. I straightened up again, and headed for the door, where I found Nikita waiting for me. He had been trailing me like a dog since he had gotten me on that plane, and I didn't exactly like what he was doing. What did he want from me? I got the horrible feeling that I knew all too well.

"It's good to see you with him again," he remarked, smiling at me. His smiles never seemed to reach his eyes, and I had no idea if he was aware of that. Had he ever really felt joy in his life? Ever really felt something close to happiness? I wanted to ask him, but that would have extended our conversation further than it needed to go, and I didn't want that.

"Yes, it is," I replied, keeping my voice as neutral as possible. "Where am I staying?"

"My room, of course," Nikita replied – and then he laughed. He must have seen how white my face had gone at the suggestion.

"Just kidding," he assured me. "We have a room for you, down the hall. This way..."

I followed him, my heart still thudding at the thought of having to share a room with him. Was he hoping I would give him a more welcoming response than that? I had no idea. I wanted to get as far away from him as I could, but I was sure he would do whatever he could to pull me back. He had plans for me, whether I liked it or not, and I didn't even want to think what they might be.

"Here you go," he told me, pushing open the door. I nodded to him in thanks and stepped into the room, pushing the door shut behind me. It had a bolt on it, thank goodness, and I shoved it over at once. It was slightly rusted and probably wouldn't hold up to much pressure, but at least it was there.

There was a bathroom attached to my room, and that was about all it had going for it – a small, old-fashioned radio was plugged into the wall, and a pile of clothes sat at the end of the bed. I doubted that any of them would actually fit me, but I didn't care, I just wanted to change out of the clothes that I had been in all this time.

I stepped into the bathroom, flicked on the slightly dim light, and started to run a bath. The taps spluttered a couple of times before they came to life, but after a moment or two, they began to fill the old claw-foot tub with water. I went to put on the radio, needing some sound in the room, something that would keep me busy.

Some tinny song started to play, one I didn't even recognize, but I didn't care. I was just glad to have something in there that wasn't the sound of my own thoughts, running through my head over and over again. I felt like I was going to lose it, lose my mind if I kept it up any longer, this attempt to run away, but I had to stick it out, at least for now.

Mauro had said there might be some chance for me to see Andreas again in the future. I had to pray that he had been telling me the truth, not just feeding me shit to try and get me to go along with what he was saying. I had no doubt that he was glad that I was out of the city, but I had no idea how Andreas felt about it.

What if what Nikita had said to me had been true? What if there was a long string of girls behind him, girls who'd had their hearts broken by that man? I had no idea if I could find the truth, one way or another, if there really had been women before me, but the way that Andreas had treated me, it was hard to believe that there could have been. He cared for me, really cared for me, in a way that nobody else had before. And I was sure that wasn't just something he could apply to some other woman now that I was gone.

I undressed, my eyes flicking back and forth to make sure that there weren't any cameras watching me – the last thing I needed right now was for Nikita to get an eyeful of my naked body, though it wasn't like I could go anywhere else even if he was. Thankfully, I was pretty sure this place was too low-tech for that.

Slipping beneath the water, I closed my eyes and tried to relax. I had no idea how I was going to pull that off, given that I was staying with a mob boss who I hated, who seemed to have designs on me for something a little more serious than just a safe-house stay, but I needed to try. I had been on for hours now, I needed to rest...

I couldn't stop thinking about Andreas. How safe I had felt when I was staying with him, how easy it had seemed when we were together. Damn, I wanted to go back in time to his apartment, lying in his arms, dozing and knowing that I had nothing at all to worry about as long as he was close to me. He was the one I knew I didn't have to worry about, the one I was certain would have protected me against anything the world threw at me – he was the one I wanted to be with right now.

Mauro had told me that Andreas wasn't going to be able to handle what came next, and that scared the shit out of me. What if something happened to him? What if he got hurt? I wished that I could be with him, show him how much I missed him and how sure I was that I could stand by his side – but it was too much danger, for me, for my father, and I knew I couldn't risk that kind of shit right now.

I closed my eyes and let my head sink back against the cool tile of the bath behind me. I could almost imagine that I was back in Andreas' luxurious bathroom. With him sitting there next to me, telling me that everything was going to be okay, that he would have done anything to take care of me. And dammit, I had wanted to believe him, more than anything in the world.

The way he looked at me, it was like he would have done anything in the world to make sure I believed him, and hell, I wished that I could. I could remember how he felt when he pulled me into his arms, when he kissed me, when he brushed his nose against mine and held me so close it was like he never wanted to let me go...

I felt my hand drifting down between my legs, almost of its own accord, and I didn't stop myself. If there was one way that I could get out of the stress in my head right now, it was with the memory of him, with the memory of the two of us together, and I intended to do just that. I focused on my fingers as they reached my clit, trying to imagine that they belonged to him instead of me, and I could picture him, behind me, hand between my legs as he played with me and kissed my neck.

"Mmm," I sighed to myself as I began to move my hand against my aching pussy. I wanted to feel the graze of his stubble against my skin, the intensity of his touch as he pulled me against him. His strong body, his breath, the way that he panted into my ear when he was as aroused as I was at that moment.

His fingers between my legs. Caressing my clit, moving in soft, slow circles around my pussy until I couldn't hold back. I squeezed my thighs tight around his imaginary hand, and felt his fingers move inside of me, pushing into my pussy so that I could feel him connect with me on that deeper level. I could almost picture his face, the way his brow would furrow slightly as he felt me pushing back against him, the way he would pant with want as he felt me grinding against his hand.

I moaned softly, biting my lip to try to hold it in, but I didn't know how the hell I could. I was thrusting back against my own hand now, picturing Andreas holding me, and it was all that I needed to get close to the edge. My entire body was starting to tense and the pleasure was beginning to build inside of me, so fast and so hard that I couldn't control it. I didn't want to – it was like all the tension that had been building this entire time was finally bursting out of me, and I wanted nothing more than to let it go, release the pressure I had been holding in.

I groaned as I felt the orgasm finally take control of me, my body trembling beneath the warm water as I came. The sound I made was nothing compared to the intensity of the orgasm that came coursing through my body as I thought of him, thought of Andreas, thought of the way that he had held me and kissed me and touched me when we had been together...

And when I came back down to Earth, it was with the blinding shock that he wasn't here anymore.

As I pulled my fingers from between my legs, the reality hit me like a ton of fucking bricks. He wasn't here. And I didn't know if he was ever going to be again.

I got myself out of the bath before I could spend much more time thinking about it. I knew that I couldn't handle the enormity of being away from him, not right now, not after everything else that had happened. Heaven only knew how hard it had been already, and I didn't want to focus on how much I had lost, how much I had left behind back in New York. How much of my life I would have to live without him, if what Mauro said had been anything close to true.

I washed my hair and climbed out of the bath quickly, pulling on the clothes that had been left out for me – they barely fit, but that didn't matter; as long as I was covered, I would be okay.

I checked to make sure that the bolt was still pushed across the door. It was, thank goodness – I didn't have to worry about someone busting in during the night to wake me. For now, all I had to do was get some sleep – and hope to hell that the memories of Andreas would start fading sooner rather than later.

Chapter Six

Andreas

I PEELED MYSELF OFF the bed and staggered to the bathroom. Now that I had seen the wound, I could feel the pain radiating all the way through the left side of my body, the shock of it coursing through my veins.

I made it to the mirror, where I pulled up my shirt and saw the edge of the bullet still sticking out of the hole in my side – it was glinting a dull gray, smeared with blood, and I knew I needed to get it out.

No time to get to a doctor. I had to act fast. I couldn't leave this building; I would have been in even more danger if I had tried to get out. This was on me. And I needed to make sure I didn't make this worse than it already was.

I dragged myself to the drinks' cart, reaching around until I found the whisky I was looking for – it was expensive shit, probably not best used for cleaning a wound, but I couldn't think of anything else right now. I tossed back a few mouthfuls myself, and then ripped open my shirt and poured a splash over the hole in my side.

"Fuck!" I cried out, as the stinging pain coursed through me. There was nobody else in the apartment to hear me complaining, but that didn't mean I was going to keep quiet. I wracked my brains for something that I could use to get it out – and my mind flashed back to Harry, one of my father's old bodyguards, boasting to me about the time he had pulled a bullet from his side in the middle of the forest.

"I sterilized some tweezers with a lighter," he had told me, after a few drinks. "Bit down on my shirt, and pulled the damn thing out."

Okay. Okay, I could manage that, right? I managed to make it back to my bathroom, where I found a lighter and a set of tweezers – not exactly high-quality medical equipment, but they would have to do for now.

I sat down on the edge of the bath, pulling off my shirt and wrapping it into a loop around my fist so I had something to bite on. Taking the tweezers, I blasted them over the lighter until they were starting to go black – that had to count, didn't it? I just needed to make sure that I wasn't jamming anything dirty in there, the last thing I needed was an infection on top of everything else that was going on. Seriously, the shit that this work called for...

My father would have been pissed to see me like this. He had wanted me to go legit, and here I was, digging a bullet out of my side in the bathroom. I didn't even remember getting hit. I would bet that this was a ricochet given that it hadn't gotten too deep into me. But damn, it still hurt like a fucking bitch, and I knew I needed to get this thing out of me before it did more damage than it already had.

I took a few deep breaths, and bit down into the shirt hard. I had no idea how long this was going to take or how hard it was going to be, but I needed to act fast. I reached down with the tweezers, and tried to grab hold of the edge of the bullet where it was sticking out of my side.

I groaned loudly into the shirt – fuck, the pain was almost too much for me to take, but I couldn't stop now. I dug around until I got a hold on the fucking thing. The blood was making it near-impossible to get a handle on pulling it out. I took a few deep breaths once I was sure that I had a good grip, and then, I yanked.

The howl I let out must have been audible even across the street, but I couldn't stop now. The pain was screaming through my system, almost more than I could take, and I panted as I tried to force myself to keep going. Every fiber of my being was telling me to stop, that this was too much for me to handle, that this was more than I could take, but I forced myself onwards. I needed to get this bullet out of me. I couldn't rely on anyone else to do it for me.

The tweezers slipped off, and I grunted, trying to find my grip again. I needed to get this over with. The blood was spurting from the wound where I had shifted the bullet, and I could already feel myself getting lightheaded. Whether it was with the blood loss or the shock, I didn't know, but frankly, I wasn't willing to wait to find out. I grasped the shiny bullet once more and yanked hard.

This time, it came out in one piece, sending a screaming jolt of pain up my side and a spurt of blood all over the bath. I yelled into the shirt again, but it was out, at least.

I managed to drag myself to my feet and make it back to the drinks' cart, where I took another few gulps of whisky and then poured it on the wound once more. Okay, that was done, at least – I had no idea if I had done anything close to a good job, but at least this was over.

I crashed down on to the couch, and the pain blinded me. I couldn't focus on anything else but the agony that was tearing at my body, couldn't think straight, couldn't even stand. I could feel the warm blood trickling down my side, and I knew that I needed to do something to stop it, but my brain was far too fuzzy to even think about something like that. I just had to keep conscious, and then I could get help once the danger had passed...

And that was the last thing that crossed my mind before the darkness swirled up to take me, and I dipped out of existence for a while.

When I came to, it was to the feeling of hands gripping my arms, and the rough shaking that Mauro was giving me to wake up.

"Andreas! Andreas, come on!"

My eyes fluttered open, and I managed to focus on the man in front of me. I frowned at him, trying to work out what he was doing shaking me like I was late for school.

"Mauro, what the fuck are you—"

"Oh, thank goodness," he sighed, and he slumped down on to the couch beside me. "I thought – I thought you were...."

He trailed off, put his head in his hands, and I instantly felt bad for putting him through this. I lifted my head, saw the streaks of blood over my body and the couch, dripping from the bathroom all the way to where I was sitting now, and winced. I couldn't exactly blame him for thinking something bad had happened.

"I'm okay," I told him, grimacing as I pulled myself upright.

"What happened?"

"I got caught by a stray bullet," I explained. "I wanted to get it out."

"And why did you do it yourself?" Mauro demanded, shaking his head. "Do you know how dangerous that is? How much trouble you could have gotten yourself into?"

"I didn't want to leave this place," I muttered, flinching as I looked him in the eye. "I wasn't sure if I was still in danger—"

"You could have put yourself in far more danger doing something as stupid as that," he muttered, and he looked down at the wound that I had left behind – it seemed to have clotted now, stopped bleeding, much to my relief, and I was feeling a whole lot less woozy than I had before. Maybe that was just the alcohol starting to wear off, or maybe I was beginning to come back down to Earth after the shock of everything that had happened.

The pain was still there, but it seemed to have dulled to a throbbing ache rather than the sharp, screaming agony that had been there before. Somehow, even though I had never done anything like that before in my life, it seemed like I had gotten away without causing myself too much trouble. I didn't know how I had pulled that off, but I would sure as fuck take it.

"You should have waited for the doctor."

"I don't know if I can trust him," I muttered. Mauro frowned at me.

"What are you talking about?"

"Look at what he let happen with Nadia's father," I pointed out. "How can we trust him when he just let him get away like that?"

Mauro's face darkened. I could tell at once there was something he didn't want to tell me – something he wished he could avoid putting into words, but he knew he had no choice but to admit to. I eyed him for a long moment, trying to work out what it might be, but I already had a sneaking suspicion that I knew.

"What is it?" I demanded. If there was one thing I was fucking sick off in all of this, it was feeling as though I didn't know what the hell was going on in my life. I was meant to be the one in charge here, so why did it feel like everything was constantly spinning out of my control?

"We need to get you to the doctor, make sure that you're not infected or anything—"

"That can wait," I told him firmly. He was meant to be the one person who I could trust in all of this, but the way that he was acting, it was telling me that I should have been more careful than I had been – that I should have played it closer to my chest. Mauro was the person I turned to in the midst of the worst times in my life, but what if he was holding something back from me? What if he was lying to me about something? And what if I couldn't get the damn truth out of him?

"You need to tell me what you're hiding," I ordered him. I expected him to dismiss me at once as paranoid, tell me that I had no idea what I was talking about right now and that I needed to drop this before it went any further. But instead, slowly, he lifted his gaze to meet mine, and I knew I was right. I knew there was something he had been keeping from me.

"I don't know if you're ready to hear it."

"Mauro," I replied, keeping my voice firm. I couldn't handle it any longer, being left out of the loop. I needed to know what was going on inside his head right now. I needed to know what he was keeping from me. I needed to know why he had been hiding so much, and I needed to know it now.

Mauro lowered his gaze for a moment, clearly gathering himself. And then, slowly, he looked back up at me, and I could finally see the scales had dropped from his eyes.

"There's something I need to tell you, Andreas," he confessed. I propped myself up on the couch, and listened to exactly what it was he had to tell me.

Chapter Seven

Nadia

WHEN I WOKE THE NEXT morning, the tears were still wet on my cheeks.

I couldn't even remember what I had been dreaming about, but I was sure that I already knew. I had gone to sleep thinking about Andreas, and I hadn't been able to get him out of my mind since. It felt like I was stuck with this constant roundabout of him, the way he made me feel, how much I missed him, and how much I wished I could see him again.

I peeled myself off the pillow and looked around. In the light of day, this place didn't look much better. There was a small, grimy window overlooking the bed, and some watery morning sunlight was easing through the glass. That must have been what woken me. Not that I had managed to get a whole lot in the way of sleep as it was.

I had been tossing and turning all night long, trying to convince myself that I just needed to pass out and rest – but that had been impossible when my ears were pricked to every sound outside my door, sure that it was Nikita trying to sneak into my room and do who knows what. The way he had been acting with me, it was obvious that he thought I owed him something, and I just had to pray it would be a while before he called in the debt.

I knew he was expecting something from me, and I wasn't naïve enough to act like I didn't know what it was. But maybe I could put off giving it to him, at least for a little while longer. I didn't want to give him the satisfaction of thinking he had me right where he wanted me, not when I was so far from home and having to fight just to keep myself together in the face of everything that was happening.

I unlatched the door and headed downstairs, the smell of something deliciously savory on the air. I was starving. I hadn't noticed until I'd caught scent of the food that was cooking, but hell, I could have eaten a full three-course meal and still been hungry.

But that thought fell right out of my head as soon as I got to the kitchen and saw my father propped up at the dining table. I rushed over to him and threw my arms around him, pulling him close.

"Oh, thank goodness, you're awake," I murmured to him, squeezing him tight.

"You might put me back to sleep if you keep crushing me this hard," he replied playfully, but he hugged me back. He was the reason I had done all of this in the first place, and I was sure he was well-aware of that – he knew that this was for him, that all of this had been for him. I just wanted him to be safe, to be happy, to be healthy, and if this was what it took to ensure that, then I would have done it a million times over.

"How are you feeling?" I fussed over him, pulling back and looking him up and down. He didn't seem too bad, but it was impossible to tell from the outside in.

"I'm all right," he replied, though I could tell from the dark rings under his eyes that it wasn't entirely true. I hoped he was going to be okay. He just needed time to rest, I was sure of it, and once he was back on his feet, we could take a look at this situation anew and work out where we were going to go from here.

"How are you?" he asked, and I took a seat next to him at the slightly-rickety table. A woman was hanging over the stove, cooking up whatever it was that had caught my nose as I came down the stairs. She smiled over at me, and I wondered if she knew who she was working for – that she was making food for the cohorts of a man who had one of the worst reputations in the entire United States of America.

"I'm okay," I lied quickly. No need to tell him I had woken up with tears on my face. He didn't need to worry about me. I knew we were both holding stuff back from each other, for the sake of taking care of each other, but I wished he would be honest. But that would require me to come out with everything that I was feeling, too, and there was no way I was going to burden him with that.

"I'm glad," he replied. I wondered if he could tell that I was lying through my teeth – I didn't doubt it. But we were lying to each other, and I supposed that was saving either of us from being called out right now. Maybe that was the way it had to be. For now, we couldn't tell the truth, because the truth was far too frightening, far too unsettling.

Nikita wasn't around, thank goodness, and I was glad I wouldn't have to deal with him leering over my shoulder this evening. The last thing I wanted was to handle his constant presence, especially his strange attempts at flirting with me. I just wanted him to leave me alone, but he didn't seem to be able to get it through his thick skull that I had no interest in him.

I supposed he wasn't used to women not being interested in him. He got what he wanted, whenever he wanted it, and I doubted I was going to be an exception to that rule. The mere thought of it sent a shiver down my spine. I wasn't going to let him get anywhere close to me, though I was sure he would do his very best to pressure me into giving him whatever he wanted. I hated the thought of what he had over me, hated the thought of giving him anything more than what I already had, but I knew he wasn't going to be quick to drop it.

"What's for breakfast?" I asked Dad, trying to keep those thoughts out of my mind. The last thing I needed was to linger too long on anything that would upset me. I'd already done plenty of that already.

"Marta is making sausages," he replied, nodding to the woman at the counter. "With sour cream and fresh bread. You remember, we used to have that on a Sunday morning with your mother all the time?"

I smiled and nodded. I did. Sometimes, it felt like he was trying his best to forget about my mother, everything that we'd been through with her, so when he brought her up, it came as something of a relief to me. Her memory was still here, maybe even more than ever, as we got closer and closer to her home country.

"Where's Nikita?" I asked, trying to keep my voice as casual as possible.

"I'm not sure, he said he would be back later today," my father replied, and he must have noticed the way my face fell when he said that, because he jumped in to make it right.

"I know you're not sure about him," he told me, gently. "But you need to at least give him a try, okay? It's not going to be easy, I understand that, but he's looking out for us. Heaven only knows how much we need that at the moment."

I didn't believe him. I didn't believe that Nikita was the only man who could help us with all of this – or if he was, I was sure it was simply because he had positioned himself in such a way that we didn't have any choice but to go along with it. I hated having to rely on him, having to rely on anyone other than myself, but hopefully he would lose interest in us sooner rather than later and leave us to our new lives here.

"I know, Dad," I promised him, and I leaned over to give him another hug. The last thing he needed right now was me making a big deal about everything that was going on. He already knew, probably all too well, just how unhappy I was at having to leave New York behind, and he wasn't going to put any more pressure on me to accept it than he already had.

We ate with Marta, who bustled around the kitchen, putting more and more food in front of me as she went. It was as though she was worried that I might drop dead on the spot if I didn't eat what she was feeding me, and honestly, I didn't blame her. I had caught sight of myself in the mirror last night, and I looked drawn, tired, spent. She probably thought I hadn't eaten in weeks.

And besides, it wasn't exactly hard to get the delicious food that she put in front of me down. Every bite reminded me of the meals that my own mother had made me growing up – simple stuff, but delicious, the sharp bite of the sour cream going perfectly with the fatty spice of the sausages. My father and I didn't speak much as we ate, but we didn't need to – there was nothing much for us to say. We were here, together, and that was all either of us cared about.

After about an hour or so, there was a creak at the door, and my head snapped up to see who it was – and sure enough, there was Nikita, looking down at the two of us with one of those cold smiles on his face.

"Good to see you eating, Nadia," he remarked. "I like a woman with a little meat on her bones."

I instantly felt my stomach turn. I didn't want to do anything that would make me more attractive to him – no, I wanted to be as repulsive to that man as humanly possible, but he was turning every little thing I did into some reason to creep all over me.

"I'm just hungry," I muttered, not daring to say more in way of argument. He wanted a woman who was going to bend over backwards and do what she was told, and I knew I needed to play at that, at least for a little while. No matter how wrong it might have felt to me.

"Well, you'll need your energy for today," he continued, reaching down to pat my shoulder. I fought the urge to pull away from him at once, wishing he would get his damn hands off of me.

"Why?" I asked.

"I'm going to take you out."

I froze.

"What are you talking about?" I blurted out, before I could stop myself. "I mean – we just got here, I need to rest—"

"Nadia, you should go," my father told me, and the hard look he was giving me told me everything that I needed to know. He wanted me out of here. He wanted to do anything he could to placate Nikita.

Nikita smiled at my father in thanks.

"Good to see you're with me, Dmitri," he remarked. "No point in keeping Nadia all cooped up in here, is there?"

"Exactly," my father agreed, and he fired a look at me as though to ensure I wasn't going to argue with him. I pressed my lips together. I didn't like how this was going, but I didn't see how I could argue, with both of them apparently intent on working against me here.

I knew I had to play along. Not just for my sake, but for my father's, too – I needed to make sure that I was able to get him through this, get him out of here in one piece. It might not be easy, but I had to try.

I smiled up at Nikita, hoping that my grin was a little more convincing than his.

"Sure thing," I told him. "I'd love to go with you. Where are we visiting?"

"Oh, you'll see when we get there," Nikita replied, cocking an eyebrow at me and letting his gaze linger on mine for a little too long. Could my father tell what this man had going through his mind? Was there anything he could have done to stop it, even if he did? I wished I could ask him if this was what he really wanted for me, but I knew that wouldn't be fair. He was just trying to survive this, and the least I could do was play fair, make it easy on both of us.

"Come on, I need to find you a helmet," Nikita continued.

"A helmet?"

"If you're going to be riding on my bike, then I want you to be safe," he told me, and he took my arm and pulled me to my feet. I wasn't going to get much of a choice with all of this. My future, at least in the immediate, had been decided for me, and the best I could do was go along without a fuss and pray nothing too awful happened while I was out.

Chapter Eight

Andreas

THE DOCTOR HOVERED over me, a look of concern on his face as he inspected the wound I had done my best to clean up; he'd just finished stitching it back together, and it looked about as healthy as it was going to get.

"Are you done?" I asked him. I wanted him out of here sooner rather than later, but I wasn't sure what I could do to make that happen. It was clear he didn't want to leave me until he was totally certain he had fixed me up, probably for fear of what would happen if he fucked up and left me hurting.

Mauro was standing just behind him, staring out of the window and on to the street below; he looked distracted, distant, and I didn't blame him. After what he had told me, I supposed it shouldn't have come as a surprise, not really.

He had gotten this doctor to the house, a different one than we normally used, which explained his nerves and his attentiveness. His hands were shaking as he cleaned up the mark on my side, and I sighed, wanting this done sooner rather than later. I knew I had to get rid of him. There was so much I needed to talk to Mauro about, and I honestly didn't even know where to begin.

"I think that should be it," the doctor told me, finally, taking a step back and snapping off the gloves that he had been wearing. "I – I think you'll be okay from here on out. Just don't do anything vigorous for the next few days, okay?"

"I'll see what I can do," I muttered. I didn't know how he expected me to sit around and do nothing after what had happened, but hey, I wasn't going to argue with him if it meant I would finally be able to get him out of here.

The doctor nodded and shot a look to Mauro, making sure he was allowed to go – Mauro waved his hand, and he practically sprinted for the exit, grabbing his bag as he did so and not looking back. Mauro tracked him all the way out of the room, and as soon as he was gone, he turned back to me.

"How are you feeling?" he asked. I shrugged, and the movement tugged on the new stiches in my side. I winced.

"It hurts," I replied. "But I'm fine. We need to talk about what we're doing next."

Mauro rubbed a hand over his face. He had tried to catch me up on as much as he could before the doctor had gotten here, telling me that he had information on Nadia and filling me in on where she had gone and what I should expect next. I was still trying to take it all in, to be honest, and was doing my very best to wrap my head around what he had told me.

"About what?"

"All of it. The Serbians, Nadia..."

"We need to start with what's happening here, in the city," he replied firmly. "That's the immediate concern right now, especially since they came after you."

"I'm fine—"

"You got shot, Andreas," Mauro told me sharply. "You can't just brush that off like it's nothing. This is serious, and I need you to start acting like it."

I gave him a look. Not a look, *the* look. I didn't need him to father me, I needed him to advise me. More than anything, though, I needed him to be honest with me, something he seemed to have been having some issues with lately.

"You sure you've told me everything I need to know?" I demanded pointedly. Mauro nodded.

"Because what you said about Nadia doesn't make any sense to me," I continued, shaking my head. "She wouldn't have just left me like that—"

"She did," Mauro replied.

"She wouldn't have gone of her own free will," I continued, not paying attention to what he had tried to interject. "She's not like that, she never has been. She would never…"

I shook my head, trailing off as I tried to wrap my head around it. I thought I knew Nadia, but if she had really just run as soon as she had gotten the chance, maybe I didn't have as much of a grasp on her as I thought. When she was with me, it had felt like the two of us had been able to be honest with one another, finally cutting to the chase and saying what needed to be said. And now, Mauro was telling me that she had fled to Serbia, with Nikita, of her own free will? That didn't make sense to me. She would never have gone with that psycho, not unless she felt as though she didn't have a choice. I was determined to find out what he had over her that made it so impossible for her to turn him down, but with her so far from me, it wasn't as though I could reach out and ask her directly.

This wasn't like when she had been in Miami before, when I had been able to keep an eye on her and make certain that she was safe even from so far away. No, she was out of my hands now, and that scared the living shit out of me. How was I going to get her back? How was I going to convince her it was safe to return? I needed to speak to her, to tell her she had nothing to worry about and she could trust me, but I got the feeling she had already made her mind up. Or she had been forced to.

"She's made her choice and that's something you need to respect," Mauro told me, firmly. "I know that you don't like it, but—"

"It's more than just not liking it," I cut him off. "I'm worried about her. I don't like what she's done, it doesn't seem like her. I think Kozlov has something over her head that he's using to get what he wants from her, and I don't like it."

"You need to focus on protecting yourself right now," he warned me. "You just got shot, for fuck's sake, you really can't pay attention to what's happening in New York right now?"

I knew he was right, but that didn't mean that I wanted to admit it. The pain nagging at my side served as a reminder of what had just happened, and I didn't much like the thought of dealing with a repeat performance. Even though I had survived this first attack, there was no certainty that I would make it through another, and I knew I had to do what I could to stick around for Nadia.

"I'm alive, that's what matters," I told him.

"I wish I had been there," Mauro muttered. "I could have done something to stop them—"

"You know that's not how it works with them," I replied. "If you had been there, you'd have just been another target for them to aim at. One of us wouldn't have made it out alive, I'm sure of it."

Mauro fell silent. He knew I was right. The more people we had on those streets, the greater the chance that one of them would end up hurt – or worse.

"I was lucky to get away with just a nick," I continued. "We need to be more careful in future. More security, more control. I don't want to give them an inch right now."

"You're right," Mauro agreed, finally. "We need to act. Do something to show them that we're not to be fucked with."

I nodded in agreement. I wasn't sure exactly what that was going to look like, but it had to come fast. The Serbians wouldn't give us much space to fuck around, and if they knew I was hurt, they would swoop in and try to make something of it. That was the last thing I needed right now. I had to put up a strong front, make sure they knew they didn't stand a chance against me. I had no idea what that was going to look like, but I knew it had to come quickly.

"How are we going to handle it?" I asked him. He knew what I was asking – should we go after them hard? Violently? Wipe them out of the city? It was everything my father had tried to work against in all the time that he had been in this business, but sometimes, the old ways were the only ones that worked.

I hated having to go against what I knew my father would have wanted, but it wasn't like we had much of a choice. He might have been planning for a move to the more legitimate side of things, but if he had seen what happened here, he wouldn't have thought twice about doing what needed to be done. Strength was the most important thing in this business, convincing everyone that you knew how to handle yourself, and if we allowed the Serbs to get away with this, we would be looking down the barrel of more serious attacks in the future.

"I've got some ideas," Mauro replied, darkly. He had been in this business long enough that he could think of all the worst ways to make sure he got what he wanted, and I intended to do everything I could to pick his brains in that regard. He could handle this, I knew he could, it was just a matter of getting the answers out of him.

"Oh, yeah?" I prompted him. "Like what?"

"I'm not sure you're going to like it."

I leaned forward, locked eyes with Mauro. Did he understand how serious this was to me right now? I had lost the woman I loved, I had gotten shot, I had dealt with all this anger and blowback from the Serbians. There wasn't anything in the world he could have said to me that would have been too far, not as far as I was concerned.

"I can handle it," I replied. "What have you got for me, Mauro?"

Chapter Nine

Nadia

AS I STEPPED OFF THE back of his bike, I knew I should have been charmed.

This was what he was doing all this for, wasn't he? To charm me? To show me that he wanted me, that he was capable of giving me everything I needed from him? He'd whisked me away from the safehouse into the sunshine of the countryside, his motorcycle whipping along the side of the Danube River as the sun beamed down on both of us. I'd had no choice but to hang on to him, even though I wanted nothing more than to pull back and hide.

I knew that, in another life, I might have been taken in by everything he was showing me. He called me beautiful, he took care of me, he looked out for my father. He was handsome, in some sort of way, with that shaven head and his beard, even if he was a good ten years older than me. In another life, maybe I would have been attracted to his hardness, his dangerous attitude, and I would have been able to forget about everything else that surrounded him.

He was trying to show me the life he thought I wanted, and I didn't have the heart to tell him that I needed no part of this. I didn't want him to romance me, because there was no way I would ever let myself fall for him.

There was someone else in my heart right now, someone who took up more space than anyone else. It would have infuriated Nikita if I had even breathed his name, so I had done my best to keep it to myself, but with every beat of my heart, I could feel him. Andreas.

I missed him so badly it felt like there was a part of me carved out and left behind, a section of me still back in New York, still lying in his bed, in his arms. I had no idea if he could even stand to think of me after the way I had run and left him behind, but even if he couldn't look me in the eye anymore, I still loved him. Loved him in a way that I had never loved anyone before in my life, loved him in a way that made everything else just vanish entirely. I wished he was here with me, that the two of us had run together so that we could be alone with one another. It was what we deserved, after everything we had been through, and yet...

"Where are we?" I asked Nikita, trying to bring myself back into the here and now. He smiled at me, almost warmly.

"This is Golubac Castle," he explained, gesturing to the magnificent, crumbling structure before us. "Normally, it's open to the public, but today it's just for us."

Alone with him? I wasn't sure I liked that idea, but I didn't have much of a choice. Short of hopping back on that bike and tearing out of there alone, I had no way to get out of this, and he must have known that. The look on his face told me everything I needed to know. He held his hand out to me, and I took it, seeing no other option but to go along with him.

"Let's take a look inside, shall we?" he murmured. This was his attempt at romance, and maybe it would have worked on someone else. I could see a million women who would have swooned at something like this, a whole castle just for the two of us, but my heart was already full with someone else.

"Yeah, sure," I replied, trying to keep a smile on my face as we headed up the stone steps to the beautiful old building.

It had been built in the fourteenth century, Nikita explained to me, and had served as a stronghold for the people who had ruled over this part of the country; it still had this nobility to it, even after all those years, the stone walls holding strong as though they would stand for eternity and a day. Even though Nikita was right there with me, I did my best to enjoy this adventure, telling myself that it might be a while until I got a chance to do something like this again.

We spiraled our way up the stairs and to the top of the fort, which looked out over the river and across the countryside below. It was a stunning view, and I wished that Andreas had been there to enjoy it with me. I could almost feel his arms wrapping around my waist, his head on my shoulder as he admired it along with me. I closed my eyes for a moment, trying to lose myself to that vision, but I knew it wouldn't last long.

And, sure enough, Nikita began to speak, shattering what was left of my fantasy entirely.

"This place is beautiful, isn't it?" he remarked, and I nodded.

"It's lovely."

"All the more beautiful for having you here, too," he remarked, and he put a hand on my waist. I fought the urge to pull away from him. Being alone with him here, I knew that I had to play along, at least a little longer. I didn't know what he would do to me if I didn't react the way he wanted me to right now, and I didn't much like the thought of finding out.

"Thanks," I replied, awkwardly. Could he tell how uncomfortable I was? He must have been able to, right? I doubted he cared. He knew that he had me exactly where he wanted me, and I was sure he was going to push to get exactly what he wanted.

"You know, people used to rule from this very spot," he continued, gesturing to the stone around us.

"They would look over everything from the safety of this fort and know that it belonged to them," Nikita explained to me. "And they would be sure they would never lose it. Don't you wish you could know what that feels like?"

I made a non-committal noise. I had no idea what he expected me to say to that, not really. I wanted to get out of here, but I knew he wasn't going to let me until he was sure that he had gotten his point through to me.

"I know what it feels like," he murmured, and he shifted a bit closer to me. I fought the urge to recoil. I hated that we were alone here right now. He seemed to have me right where he wanted me. If I could have pushed him away, I would have, but I didn't have a choice. For the safety of myself and my father, I had to let him think I was okay with this.

"But I want someone to share it with, Nadia," he continued, reaching out to touch my hand. My fingers hung limply in his, not providing any encouragement. I didn't want to give him an inch.

"I want a bride."

His words hung in the air between us, and I tried not to let the panic take control of me. He was going to force me to accept this, and I wasn't sure I could go through with it. I knew that Mauro had told me to go along with anything he asked, but this...

"I'm sure that this comes as a shock to you," he went on. "But your beauty has entranced me from the day we met, Nadia. I can't imagine sharing all of this with anyone other than you, I hope you understand that."

He caught my face in his hand and brought it around so that I had no choice but to look at him. His fingers were firm on my skin, and it was clear he was telling me I was meant to be paying attention to him right now.

"I know that you'll be the perfect wife for me, Nadia," he told me. "I want to show you everything that you can have if you stay with me. Do you know how good life could be, if you just agree to what I'm asking?"

It was like he was striking a business deal, not making a proposal. I eyed him for a long moment. I wasn't sure how to respond. My gut was telling me to wrench myself away from him, fling myself over the edge of the fort if that's what it took, and flee as far as I could from this man, but I had to stay put. I dragged my eyes from his, praying that he wasn't going to ask me to make a decision right now.

"And I know my life would be a lot easier if you agreed," he continued, his voice taking on that edge that told me that I should look out for myself.

"What do you mean?" I asked him.

"Well, my anger at the people who've wronged me back in America might not feel as... pressing if I had the support of a woman like you," he told me. I stared at him.

"I don't know what you—"

"Take someone like Andreas, for example," he replied, waving his hand. "After everything he's done, you'd expect me to take him out."

My heart skipped a beat inside my chest. I hated hearing him even talk about Andreas, but I knew this was a power-play. He was trying to get me to agree to anything he put out there by scaring me shitless. I kept my face as neutral as I could, praying that I wasn't giving anything away before I was ready.

"But if I had someone like you to soothe me, I might feel differently," he explained. "And I might be willing to forget he ever wronged me in the first place. Do you know what I mean?"

"I do," I murmured. He was holding Andreas' life over my head, making me responsible for anything that happened to him. My gut reaction was to do whatever it took to protect the man I loved – but would he want me to go through with whatever he was suggesting? Would he really want me to marry this man, just to keep him safe?

"And I hope that you'll see how important it is to me," he went on. "And perhaps that could have some... influence on your decision."

He was blackmailing me. Blackmailing me with the life of Andreas because he knew he could. My father's life was in his hands, too, but they had formed some sort of truce where nothing could happen to my dad as long as he was here. Andreas, though? Nikita had no reason to treat him with the same respect. He and Andreas were rivals, not just in business, but now over me – and he was going to use that to twist the knife and get me to go along with what he was suggesting.

Marriage, though. Something as huge as that... I didn't know that I could handle it. A whole life with this man? I mean, yes, he might not live a whole lot of it, given his line of work, but still – there was so much I would have to go through, so much I would have to endure. I could still feel the grip of his hands on my face, the sick sensation that his touch stirred in me. Could I go through with something more than that? I wasn't sure I could. I wasn't sure that I could even entertain the idea of it.

"You see what I'm saying?" he asked, and I nodded.

"I do."

"I like to hear you say those words," he murmured, and that smile licked up his lips again. A smile, like he was a predator who had just spotted unattended prey at loose in the woods. I shivered. It wasn't cold up there on the fort, but he seemed to bring with him this air of freezing ice, like he was solidifying everything to snow around him.

"I... this is all so much," I told him quickly. I wanted to make out like I was flustered by a proposal as huge as that, but I had no idea how he would take it. He wasn't a man who was used to being told no, and I needed to frame this in just the right way to convince him I was so stunned by the romance of this gesture that I needed time to think.

"I know," he murmured. "But when you know, you know. And I know about you, Nadia. I'm sure about you."

I chewed on my lip. How was I meant to get out of this? He was standing there in front of me, basically telling me that he would kill Andreas if I didn't give him what he wanted, and I needed to come up with an answer or he was going to take the last thing that I was hanging on to from me.

"This could all be ours," he told me, sweeping his hand out over the scenery in front of us. "We could rule together. You, by my side..."

"I don't know if I'm ready for that," I blurted out, finally. It was the closest I could come to telling him that he was fucking crazy if he thought I was going to go along with his scheme for an instant – the closest I could come without being stranded out here after he drove off in a fury, that was. I had to be tactical. My mind was spinning, trying to come up with some way that I could shut this all down.

A frown crossed his face for a moment, but he didn't let my discomfort throw him.

"Well, I'm sure I can give you some time to think about it," he reasoned. "Say... twenty-four hours?"

I winced. Not anywhere close to enough, but if that was all that he was going to give me, I would have to hope that I could make it work. I nodded.

"Thank you," I breathed. It wasn't long, but it was better than nothing, and I would take anything I could get right now.

"You could be my Danube, Nadia," Nikita told me, as he wrapped his arms around me, pulling me close. The smell of his skin filled my nostrils, and I fought the urge to pull back and shove him away.

"Running through everything that I do," he murmured. "Just think about it. You and me, against the world. Doesn't that sound perfect?"

I didn't reply. Because I knew that no answer I gave would be convincing enough for him – and I didn't want to risk more than I already had in making sure I got out of here in one piece.

Chapter Ten

Andreas

AS I SAT IN THE CAR, listening to the sound of gunfire and the cries of suffering from inside the building, I wondered what my father would have made of all of this.

He had always done what needed to be done. That was what I was trying to see through right now; if the Serbs wanted a fight, then I would give it to them. My father was ruthless when he needed to be, even if he had tried to keep most of that from me. I was sure he would have responded to violence with violence of his own.

Mauro and I had put the plan together the night before, thrown everything into place so we could put it all into action today. We didn't have long before the Serbians came looking for another piece of me, and we had to act fast. We had tracked down the building where Nikita ran most of his operations, and right now, a dozen or so of my men were working their way through it, clearing it of guards and allies so I had a clear run to the top.

I had no idea if Nikita was even there right now. That didn't matter. Whoever it was who I got my hands on, they would understand the message I was trying to get across. It had been a long time since we'd had to use such violent tactics to get what we wanted, but I had to do what needed to be done. If I didn't take them out, then they were going to come swinging for me, and there wasn't a chance in hell that I was going to let them do that.

The bullet wound was still nagging in my side, but it had started to heal. The doctor had done a good job patching me up, much to my relief, and I knew I would make it out the other side in one piece. Which was more than could be said for most of the guys in that building.

A twinge of guilt nagged at the back of my mind. My father had wanted us to move to a more legitimate form of business, and here I was, committing a fucking massacre. But this was about protecting our territory, protecting my life. If we didn't strike out, then there was no telling what might happen next, and we couldn't take that risk. We needed to be able to stand up and fight, otherwise the Serbs would roll right over us and we would have nothing left at all.

I was protecting my father's legacy. I wasn't going to let anyone destroy what he had worked so hard to build. He might not have wanted this for me, but that wasn't how it worked. Sometimes, you had to do shit you thought you would never have to do, and I was just taking care of what needed to be done.

Mauro had come with me today. I didn't blame him. He wanted to be present for all of this. Even now, the sound of gunfire burned itself into my mind, a reminder of the chaos that had erupted at the club when I had been there, when the attack had come against me. I had been lucky to make it out of there alive, and I was certain they wouldn't let me get away again so easily.

By the time things started to calm down and the noise began to dissipate, I climbed out of the car. The building we had attacked was nondescript, would have passed for any other warehouse in the business district, but I knew better. What happened inside there was bigger and more dangerous than almost anything else in this city, and that was saying something.

I had wanted to go in there to fight myself, but Mauro had told me in no uncertain terms that he wasn't going to let that happen.

"It's too dangerous," he had told me. "We need you there to show them that they can't fuck with your family. If your dead, that's not exactly going to work."

"I get it," I muttered, but I hated being left out of the loop like this. I hated having to accept that I was too important to get hurt any more than I already had. I had been taking a huge risk going to that meeting in the first place, and look where it had gotten me – a bullet buried in my side.

I waited until the gunfire had dropped off, and there was a buzz on the radio that the guys had left me. They had told me that they were going to get in touch when they had cleared the building. It sounded to me like they had managed it, but of course, it was impossible to tell. I had no idea how it might have gone.

"We're clear, boss," a gruff voice came down the line. It sounded like Leon, the head of security, who had told me that he would get this under control in no time.

"I'm safe to come in?"

"I'm coming down to meet you at the entrance now."

We headed to the door, and tried to steel myself for what I was about to see. It wasn't as though I hadn't seen plenty of shit in my time in this business, but that didn't mean I was any more used to laying eyes on the kind of carnage that I knew my men would have had to leave behind.

Leon was waiting for me by the time I got to the door, and I could smell the thick, metallic scent of blood on the air before I so much as stepped inside. I followed him wordlessly into the building, and my eyes darted back and forth as I took in the piles of dead bodies around us. A dozen? More? I didn't know how many guards and other personnel they kept around here, but the floors seemed to be piled high with them.

Bodies were sprawled everywhere, even as I continued up the stairs towards the top of the building. I knew I should have expected it, but still – this much bloodshed, this much violence, it was something I knew my father had wanted me to avoid.

But sometimes, you couldn't. Sometimes, you had to be ready to fight for what you believed in. And I believed that our empire deserved to survive. Mauro didn't seem bothered by any of it, but I was sure he had seen worse in his time working for my father. Something in him was steely, hardened, and he wasn't going to let anything like this bother him.

By the time we reached the top of the stairs, facing the small office that two of my guards were standing outside, I prepared myself for what was inside. I had asked them to capture whoever they could find who seemed important – we needed some leverage, something to work with when it came to Nikita.

I pushed the door open, Mauro close behind me, and stepped inside. Bound and bloodied, but alive, on a chair in front of me was a man I recognized – his resemblance to Nikita was so strong that for a moment I thought we had managed to take the boss, but no. It was his brother, Mikhail, his head of security – the one they called the Butcher on the streets.

Not that he looked up to much now. His head was lolling down to his chest, his hands bound behind the chair that he was sitting on. I was glad they had left him alive – we might be able to get something out of him in this state. I had no idea where to start, but as long as we had him, we had something over Nikita. A foothold.

"You understand why we kept you alive?" I barked at him. He nodded, a grin spreading over his battered face.

"Of course I do," he croaked back, his voice bubbling with blood as he tried to get the words out. Even though all the odds were against him, he seemed to be enjoying this on some level. I didn't like that, not one little bit, but I brushed it off and stayed focused.

"Good, then you understand that we could turn you in to the cops any moment," I warned him. "You know how much they have on you, right? How much you're accused of?"

He nodded, slowly, blood dripping from his bottom lip and staining his white shirt. His eyes held that same cold, diffident expression as Nikita's, the family resemblance impossible to ignore.

"Oh, I know," he replied. "I'd tell them all about it myself, if I could."

"How are you not ashamed of any of it?" I asked him. He shrugged.

"Nothing to be ashamed of."

"You're not scared of what's going to happen to you?" I pressed. Even though he was putting on a good act, I was sure that something must be getting under his skin – but if it was, he was hiding it well, and I needed to know what he had to fall back on that he was so sure would protect him.

"Of course not," he replied, spitting out a mouthful of blood on to the floor. "Why should I be?"

His eyes slid past me, and towards Mauro. That smile passed over his face again.

I turned, and saw that Mauro was holding a gun – pointing it straight at Mikhail. What the fuck was happening? He was never violent, he was my advisor—

I turned back to Mikhail just in time to watch his face drop as Mauro pulled the trigger, the bullet passing straight through Mikhail's head and sending him crashing on to the floor. I spun around to face Mauro, panic shooting through me, but before I could say another word, he grabbed me and pushed me down.

"Duck!" he yelled, and I looked up just in time to see one of the guards – one of *my* guards – unloading a gun exactly where I had been standing a moment before. Mauro let off a shot at him, and made contact with his shoulder, but the guard got a shot off at Mauro, clipping him before he slid to the ground.

I felt a hand on the back of my neck, pulling me upright. I had no idea what was going on, the sound of the gunfire ringing in my ears as I was dragged out of the office, Mauro hot on my tail. What the fuck had just happened? Why was Mauro shooting? Why was one of my own guards firing at us? What the hell had gone down that I didn't know about?

We stumbled back into the light again, and the smell of smoke choked my senses. I turned, to see a couple of my men setting fire to the building that we had just left behind. Mauro was with me, though his face was pale and he was carrying weight uncomfortably from where he had been clipped.

"Let's get the fuck out of here," he rasped at me, and he pulled me towards the car – and, hopefully, towards a little more clarity. Because I was utterly out of the loop here, and if there was one thing I hated, it was feeling as though I didn't have a clue what was going on.

Chapter Eleven

Nadia

I TUCKED MY KNEES UP to my chest, my throat raw from the sobbing I had been doing since I had gotten back, and tried, once again, to work out what the fuck I was going to do next.

I didn't have any idea, not really. I had been thinking about it since Nikita had driven me back to the house, since he had put that time-limit on how long I had to make my choice. Twenty-four hours, and he was expecting an answer, and I knew that I couldn't give him anything less than what he wanted.

I had buried my head in my pillow and just cried and cried and cried at first. He knew he had me right where he wanted me, and that he could get anything he needed out of me. If he had to have a wife, then he was going to make me into just that. I hated myself for thinking I wouldn't get pulled into something darker than I could handle, but how could I have known he would want this? I was certain he had just been using me to hurt Andreas, but now, he seemed determined to prove once and for all that I was his woman.

Maybe he just wanted to get one over on Andreas. Prove that there was nothing he couldn't take from him, even me. What if Andreas really thought I wanted to go through with this? That I had left him for a man like Nikita? Shit, I wished I could talk to him, show him that I missed him, how much I wanted to be with him right now. I was certain he would do everything he could to get me out of this mess if he knew about it, but there was nothing he could pull off from so far away.

71

I needed him right now, more than ever. Mauro had promised me there might be a day in the future when we could be together again, but if I was Nikita's wife, how the fuck was that going to happen? I was going to be married to his greatest enemy, and he would never be able to so much as look at me again without incurring the wrath of my new husband-to-be.

A woman on the brink of getting engaged should be happy, excited, but all I could think about was fear. What would happen if I said no to him? It wasn't even an option. He would take me out the moment I didn't give him what he wanted, and I doubted he would hesitate to do the same to my father, too. All of this was hinging on me.

No wasn't an option. So what if I said yes? What then? What could I do to keep myself safe? I couldn't stand the thought of pretending to care for him for even a second, but I didn't have a choice. If I turned him down, he would kill me, I was sure of it. But there had to be a way around saying yes – a way around actually committing myself to him in the way that he wanted me to.

But what was it? I wracked my brains. I wanted him gone, but I couldn't think of a way to make it happen. How was I supposed to save myself, save my father? The only way I could ensure that was if I took Nikita out of the equation entirely, but I couldn't do it myself.

Could I?

My mind started to race. If he trusted me, if he really believed I wanted to marry him, maybe he would start to let his guard down. And if he let his guard down, I could use that to lash out at him. I would have to play the dutiful fiancée and wife for a while, the thought of which made me sick, but if I did it for long enough...

He would start to believe that it was real. And I could hit him with the last thing he expected.

It would have to be something subtle, something he wouldn't think to check for. Poison? That would make the most sense. I could play at being the housewife, wanting to care for him and cook for him, and slip something into his drink that he wouldn't be able to survive.

The thought of it made my heart pound. I had never killed someone, and I had never thought I would. But if this was the only way I would be able to protect myself from Nikita – protect myself, and the people around me – I didn't have much of a choice.

I rose to my feet and washed my face in the bathroom, looked at myself in the mirror. I could do this. More than that – I had to do it. I had to be able to see this through, no matter how much it scared me, no matter how much I wished I wasn't stuck in this nightmare.

I hardly even recognized myself. What kind of person would come up with the plan I had just conceived of in my head? What kind of person could go through with an actual fucking murder?

The kind who had been backed into a corner they couldn't get out of, that's what. I didn't have a choice. It was this, or lose everyone who mattered to me, and there was no way I was going to let that happen.

I went back to bed and stared at the ceiling. Even though I was scared, a strange sense of calm settled over me, too – something peaceful, comfortable. I could do this. If I had to, I could do this, and I would come out the other side in one piece and make sure that I didn't get trapped in a marriage with that awful man. He might have thought he had won for now, but he hadn't. I could take him down. I could take him out.

I pulled the covers over myself, and soon, I drifted off to sleep. The calm was a relief, after all the sadness and terror that had consumed me before. I still didn't know if I could do it, but I was willing to try, and that was more than I had imagined I would get close to before now.

When I woke the next morning, it was after a dreamless sleep, and I rose from the bed to get dressed and wash up. From this moment onward, I had to be willing to play the role of his lover – whatever that took. I had to convince him so he trusted me completely. The thought of what he might ask from me to prove my loyalty made my stomach turn, but I didn't let it show on my face. This was going to be the performance of a lifetime, and I was going to survive it.

I headed downstairs, where my father was already eating breakfast. I dropped a kiss on top of his head, a reminder of why I was doing all of this in the first place. He had already been through enough as it was, and he deserved a chance to live the life he wanted to. I would keep him safe. I would do anything I could to make sure he survived this, and that the two of us could go back to the life we had known before.

"You're in a good mood today," he remarked, smiling up at me. I nodded.

"Yes, I am," I replied. "I've... I'm feeling better about everything."

"I'm glad to hear that," he told me, and he reached out to squeeze my shoulder. He just wanted me to be happy, that was why he had done all of this. Little did he know that I was about to agree to something that would make me more miserable than I could imagine, in the name of making sure both of us came out of this in one piece.

I poured myself a coffee and sat at the table, chatting to my father about the trip I had taken the day before. I had rushed off to my room before I'd had a chance to talk to anyone about what had happened, too terrified and tearful to even think about putting a good spin on it, but my PR campaign started here and now – with my dad.

I hated lying to him, but if that's what it took, I would do it. We had been through so much as it was already, and there was no way that I was going to put him through anything more. If he knew I was submitting myself to a marriage that I didn't want to be a part of, I knew he would freak out and do his best to pull me out of it. He needed to believe I was going through with this because I really, truly wanted to, even if that was a lie in more ways than I could count.

"It sounds beautiful," My father remarked. "Your mother and I used to picnic by the Danube when we were first together..."

"I can see why," I replied, smiling at the thought of them together. "It's beautiful."

"Almost as beautiful as your mother was," he replied, a little wistful. I loved hearing him talk about her. And I hoped, one day, that I would be with someone who I could talk about with that same love that he did.

Before I could get out another word, though, Nikita marched into the kitchen. He leaned down to drop a kiss on my cheek, and I fought the urge to pull away from him, smiling up at him sweetly instead.

"Good morning," I greeted him, lifting my voice to this cartoon-princess sweetness and hoping that he believed it.

"Good morning," he replied. "Feeling better?"

I had told him that I was ill from the drive the night before, praying that he would leave me alone, but today, I nodded.

"Much," I cooed sweetly. "It's good to see you again, Nikita."

"I'll give the two of you some privacy," my father remarked, rising to his feet and heading to the door. He seemed to be feeling much better these days, but the treatment he had been receiving could be rescinded at a moment's notice. Nikita didn't even have to say any of that out loud, I just knew it to be true. He liked having that power over the people around him, likely because he knew none of them would choose to spend time with him if that wasn't the case.

"I've been thinking about your offer yesterday," I told him, my heart pounding in my chest. I needed to convince him, now more than ever, but I could hardly keep the venom or disgust out of my voice as I spoke.

"I'm glad to hear it," he replied, as he turned to face me again. I could still feel his lips on my cheek. I would have to get used to it, if I was going to go through with this. I could do it – I could. I had to.

"And I think you're right," I admitted. "I... we would be good together. We should... get married."

I had to choke the words out of my mouth, hoped that he would mistake it for the emotion of a woman who had just said yes to a proposal. But truly, I knew he didn't care what I thought about this. As long as he got what he wanted, he would be happy.

And, sure enough, the grin that spread over his face told me everything I needed to know. He didn't care how I felt about it. He cared that I had agreed to his sick little plan. He nodded.

"We'll go back to New York, and we can rule together," he told me. "You, by my side. Just like that fortress. The two of us against the world..."

I let him talk. I was going to have to get used to hearing him go on and on like that if we were going to be married. I could handle it.

I could handle anything, as long as it meant that the people I loved stayed safe and alive.

Chapter Twelve

Andreas

"CAN'T YOU WORK ANY faster?" I demanded, as the doctor hovered over Mauro and tried to remove the bullet from his shoulder. Mauro winced, biting back the pain that I knew he had to be feeling right now.

"I'm going as fast as I can—"

"Not fast enough," I warned him, pacing back and forth in front of the armchair in my apartment as I waited for him to finish up.

Mauro and I had just made it back from the attack on Nikita's building, and I was still reeling from the mess of everything that had happened. Where the fuck was I even meant to start? The chaos that had unfolded was still cluttered in my mind, and I couldn't sort through any of it until I was able to speak to Mauro about what he knew.

"I'm not even a doctor, I'm a vet," the guy protested. He was the same doctor who had removed the bullet from me, the one Mauro had managed to come up with to take care of my wounds.

"Yes, and you owe us big time," Mauro growled at him through gritted teeth. "So get that thing *out* of there before we double your debt."

He went back to work, and I watched with concern. I knew the wound might not have looked immediately dangerous, but Mauro was an older guy now and if we weren't careful, he could wind up with a serious injury.

We had gotten out of there in one piece, that had to count for something. I just needed to understand what the fuck had happened to cause my own men to turn on me like that. Were they working with Nikita? Why had Mikhail seemed so confident in the way that he had spoken to me? Did he know Mauro? Did Mauro work with him at some point in the past? I needed answers, but until we had Mauro safe again, I couldn't focus on getting them.

The doctor hunched over the wound and reached in with a pair of tweezers, and finally managed to yank out the bullet – a spray of blood followed, dribbling down Mauro's back, and he grunted with discomfort.

"How does it feel?" I asked him.

"Fucking painful," Mauro replied, though he was doing his best not to let it show on his face. He never wanted anyone to see weakness in him, I had known him long enough to be aware of that. The doctor pressed a sterilized swab against the wound until the bleeding started to slow down, and then carefully papered over it with a dressing that would keep it safe for the time being.

"That should be it," he told us, straightening up again. His hands were still shaking as he put away his equipment.

"Thank you," Mauro replied. "Now, leave us. I need to talk to Andreas."

The doctor didn't need telling twice, and he practically sprinted to the door to get the hell out of there before anything else could happen. Mauro turned to me, and I saw him press his hand to his stomach.

"Did you get caught again?" I asked him, nodding to the pressure his fingers were applying. He shook his head.

"It's not important."

"What do you mean? We need to get the doctor back in here—"

"Andreas, I don't have much time," Mauro told me, urgently, and the tone to his voice made me stop dead in my tracks. Much time for – for what?

"Did you get hit?"

"Listen to me," he ordered as he sank back on to the chair behind him. "I – I don't have long. I need to tell you everything."

"What's everything?" I asked. His face was paling, and he closed his eyes. I could see blood leaking through his fingers, a sure sign that it was serious.

"I've been working for someone else," he admitted. The fact that he wasn't looking at me seemed to make it easier for him. My heart dropped in my chest.

"What do you mean?"

"The FBI," he confessed, blurting the words out as though they came from some place deep inside of him. "I've been – I've been with them since the start."

My jaw dropped. There was no way – Mauro? I had been working with him for years, so had my father. We had trusted him with so much, and now...

"Listen to me!" he barked, seeing me drifting in front of him. "I – I was working with your father to try and get him out of the business. I started out trying to take him down, but as more time passed, it became obvious that I should pivot him to something legit. That way, I could keep his connections without losing his status."

He took a deep, ragged breath. I was too stunned to say anything.

"We thought we could make this work, but the Serbians have always been there to pull him and you back in," he continued. "We wanted to get you out, get you both out, but they – they're never going to let that happen. You're their scapegoat, and it's going to stay that way as long as you keep engaging with them. Nikita—"

He caught his breath again, groaning with discomfort, and I planted my hand over his to try and stem the flow of warm blood. It was useless. Why hadn't he let us treat him? Was he already too far gone?

"Nikita took Nadia to Serbia. We're sure that he's going to try and marry her, so that he can consolidate his power," he explained. "He thinks that he'll have beaten you if he marries her. I don't know what he's going to use to make sure of it, but he's not going to hold anything back to make sure he gets her where he wants her."

I felt physically sick at the thought of Nadia with that man. No way was I going to let that happen. No way.

"How do you know this?" I asked him, urgently. I knew time was running short. I didn't want to waste a moment of it. Mauro shook his head.

"We have agents working with the Serbs too," he explained, his voice starting to fade. "They told me – they've been keeping up with what's going on there, passing it back to me."

He reached out to grasp my arm, smearing my skin with his blood. His eyes were starting to get hazy and I knew I didn't have much time left with him.

"You need to get her out of there," he continued, as best he could. "They'll come back to New York to get married, and you have to be ready when they do."

"Ready for what?"

"War," he replied. "All-out war. If you want to stop Nikita and save Nadia and her father, you have to be ready to go to war—"

He coughed violently, spraying a mixture of saliva and blood over the couch. I couldn't believe this was happening. I was going to lose him. This man who had been there my entire life, I was going to lose him – right after I found out that he had lied to me about pretty much every single thing that had marked out our life together.

"Listen to me," he urged me. "You can win this. You just have to be ready to take him on. He expects you to fold, but you don't have to. You can fight. You can beat him. You need to. It's the only way the Serbs are going to stop. Get rid of Nikita, cut off the head, and you can end them for good."

"I need you there with me," I told him urgently. "Mauro, you know I can't do this without you—"

"You can," he breathed back. "I know you can. You're more capable than you think. I'm just…"

He trailed off. His eyes were starting to grow distant. He was losing his grip on reality. How had he gotten hit and I hadn't noticed? How had I let this happen? How hadn't I known about his… about his real affiliation?

"I'm going," he admitted, finally. I shook my head.

"You can't," I snapped at him, almost angry. "You can't, Mauro, listen to yourself. There's too much left to tell me."

"I have notes, you can find them," he explained, voice raspy and distant. "You can talk to the agents who were on my case, they'll tell you as much as they can…"

I wanted to shake him, but I knew it wasn't going to work. He was an old man now. An old man who had spent most of his life trying to help my family, even if we hadn't known it at the time. I could feel the tears catching at the back of my throat, tried to swallow them down, but there was no point. I had to find a way to bring him back, even as he was drifting from me.

"Mauro," I pleaded with him, but he shook his head.

"My part is over," he told me, and there was a sudden serenity to his voice, as though he had utterly accepted what was going through his mind.

"You can't leave me to do this alone," I begged him. He closed his eyes again.

"You're stronger than you think, Andreas," he assured me, and with that, I watched as the last vestiges of life dripped out of him. The blood that had been dribbling from the wound in his side started to ease up, the flow slowing as his heartbeat faded away to nothing, and I knew I had lost him.

I had lost the one connection I still had left to my father. The one person who had been there through all of it. The one person, apparently, who had been lying to us all of this time, keeping back the truth when he should have been sharing it.

I stared at him for a long time, just sitting there on the ground in front of him. Was what he had told me true? Could it be? I was sure there had to be something more to all of this, something I was missing, but for now, all I had to go on was what he had told me.

And what he had told me was that there was good reason to be worried about Nadia. That I would have to step up and make sure she didn't get snatched by Nikita. Did he really want to marry her? The thought of his hands on her was enough to make me feel ill, but I ignored it. I had to act fast.

If there was really war on the way, I had to be ready to ride at dawn. And I would be. Just as soon as I had laid Mauro to rest – and just as soon as I had found out how much of this story that he had told me was true.

Chapter Thirteen

Nadia

AS WE HEADED TOWARDS the plane, I felt my stomach twist with excitement.

I couldn't believe we were really going back to New York. I had thought the wedding would take place in Serbia, but Nikita had been insistent – he wanted all of his family to be there, as much of the Serbian community as he could convince to attend.

I had no doubt it would be a lavish affair. It was the kind of wedding that would go down in the history books. Nikita would make sure of that – I knew he would do anything in his power to ensure that he proved he had me all to himself, no matter how much I wished he would leave me the fuck alone for good.

But New York – New York would, at least, bring me a lot closer to Andreas. And if I was closer to Andreas, then I might be able to pull off this crazy plan that I had been working on since the moment I had come to terms with the marriage I'd agreed to.

Nikita had insisted on pushing it through as quickly as he could. Not that I was surprised by it; he must have known that his grip on me was tenuous at best, and if he gave me an instant to think about what I was doing, I would find a way to back out of it.

"I know you'll be so happy as my wife," he told me as we packed up what little things we had here so we could head back to New York. We had just flown out from there, but hell, I wasn't going to point out how stupid this all was. If Nikita wanted to take me back to my home city, I needed to go along with him.

"Me too," I replied, sugaring my words as best I could. I had no idea how I was going to keep his hands off of me, but I would find a way. Maybe by playing demure? I got the feeling he was old-fashioned and would want a wife in the same vein, and perhaps I could take advantage of that right now.

Of course, I was anything but demure, in my own head, at least. I found my mind drifting to Andreas constantly. I wanted him so badly, it almost hurt. I could feel the desire for him pulsing in my system, especially when I lay awake at night. Hell, if he were there next to me, there was nothing I wouldn't have done to him. I wanted to taste every inch of his body, feel the passion between us again. Nothing else came close. Nothing else could.

But, as far as Nikita was concerned, I was focused on nothing but our forthcoming nuptials – and I intended to keep it that way. He was already putting things in motion, planning with calls back to the city, and by the sounds of it, he was already distracted from me by the thought of our marriage. I hoped it stayed that way.

There were a few days between my acceptance of his proposal and our return to New York, but it felt like a lifetime. My father seemed as pleased as I was, though still a little nervous.

"Are you sure this is what you want to do?" he had asked me, taking me aside one afternoon after I had accepted Nikita's proposal. I nodded.

"It makes sense," I told him. I needed him to believe I wanted this – needed him to buy into the story that I was spinning, even if I didn't want a single part of it. That was the closest I could come to giving him an answer which was anything near truthful. He would be able to see through me if I just straight-up lied to him.

He smiled at me – I knew he wasn't sure about this, but he was doing his best to convince himself that it had all worked out. He likely knew as well as I did that there was no way that Nikita was going to let us leave if I didn't agree to his proposal. He thought he had me right where he wanted me, and all I could do was run along with it and hope for the best.

The plane back to New York was as luxurious and glamorous as the one out had been, but this time, I didn't feel the same sense of dread I had when we had been leaving for Serbia. No, this was going to bring me closer to home, closer to Andreas – closer to freedom from all of this. And that was all that mattered.

Nikita sat next to me as I peered out of the window, trying to studiously ignore his attempts to get me to engage with him. Just because I had agreed to marry him didn't mean that I suddenly had to be hanging on his every word. If he had something to say about it, I would just brush it off as pre-wedding nerves and pray he didn't delve any deeper than that.

He reached to drape his arm around the back of my chair. He was getting far too comfortable with me, but I'd have to get used to it. I turned to him and smiled, hoping that it looked genuine.

"Are you looking forward to getting back to New York?" I enquired. My voice sounded robotic, even to my own ears, but he didn't seem to notice. I doubted he cared much, anyway. He seemed the type who was more interested in the sound of his own voice than anything else.

"I'm looking forward to showing everyone my new wife," he replied, cocking an eyebrow at me. I felt my stomach flip. The thought of him being able to call me that was enough to make me want to vomit, but I pushed it down. I had to be convincing. I had to make sure that I proved to him that he could trust me.

So when I pulled the trigger – or rather, dripped the poison into his drink – he would never in a million years see it coming.

"Yes, the wedding's going to be fun," I replied.

"I'm more interested in the wedding night," he murmured, leaning in a little closer. I could smell his breath between us, and I jerked back without thinking. A flash of anger crossed his face, and I had to think fast to come up with a good reason as to why I didn't want my fiancé to kiss me.

"I'd rather save all of that until our wedding night," I told him, biting my lip and smiling as sweetly as I could. I was sure he knew I was far from a virgin, but I needed him to believe it for now.

"Really?" he replied, sounding irritated. I nodded.

"If we're going to do this, then we're going to do it properly," I replied firmly. Would he believe that? I was trying to be the woman I thought he'd want to marry, demure and innocent. After a pause, he nodded.

"Of course," he replied. "Whatever you want. If I can restrain myself that long."

"If you can," I quickly added. "I'll make sure that our wedding night is the best of your entire life..."

I trailed off, allowing his mind to fill in the blanks that he wanted to, and I saw his eyes light up. I hated to think what he was imagining at that moment, but I couldn't let it get under my skin. I was never going to go through with it, anyway – let him think what he wanted, it wasn't going to change a damn thing.

"I'll look forward to it," he replied, and he reached out to cover my hand with his own for the rest of the flight.

I hated feeling the heat of his skin on mine, but it wasn't as though I had a choice right now. I needed to go along with what he was doing, and I needed him to believe that I had truly changed my mind and decided that marrying him was the best thing that I could possibly do.

My father was sitting opposite us, dozing in his chair, a pair of headphones cutting him off from the rest of the world. Though he seemed better than he had a few days ago, I knew he was still weak, and all this travel wouldn't do much to help him. I needed to keep focused on what I had to do, for his sake as much as mine. I needed to ensure that Nikita believed me, because my father's life depended on it, and nothing was going to stop me from rescuing him.

The plane hurtled through the sky and Nikita gripped my hand as though he was making some kind of point. What it was, I didn't care to find out.

I just had to get through the next few days, and convince him that I meant him no harm. Convince him that I couldn't wait to be his wife and rule alongside him the way that he wanted me to. And then, when the time was right – I would strike. And take Nikita down for good.

Chapter Fourteen

Andreas

I WATCHED AS THE CORONER rolled Mauro's body out of the apartment. My entire system was riddled with so much shock, it was as though it was happening to someone else entirely.

Because there was no way that Mauro could be dead. There just wasn't. He had always been around, as long as I could remember, had always been a part of my life. And he wasn't just gone – he was gone on the heels of the revelation that he hadn't been who he said he was.

Had he been telling the truth? There was no way he would have lied to me. No way he would have made the last things he'd said to me untrue. Would he? Surely not. My mind was spinning as I tried to make it all fit together, but I just couldn't come close. My brain was spent from everything that had happened, and now – now that he was gone – I had to reckon with what he had left behind.

His blood was still staining the armchair and the floor in front of it, and I stepped over it to grab his phone. I had pulled it from his pocket before he had been taken out of here. I was sure there would be something on here that I could use, no matter how much I wished I didn't have to. No matter how much I wished he was here to guide me.

I had never been out on my own like this before, and it scared me. It was the buzzing, fizzing kind of fear that warned me that I might not be able to take this on. But I had to. If I was going to stop Nikita, and if I was going to be able to keep Nadia safe, then I needed to be able to fight right now, fight harder than I ever had before.

I sat down on the edge of the couch and started going through Mauro's phone; he had never bothered locking it. Probably because he had no reason to think that my father or I would ever go looking for anything in it. We had trusted him so much, it hadn't even crossed either of our minds in all the time that he had been working for us that he might be pulling for a different side.

I wasn't sure I believed him. I didn't know why he would lie to me like that, sure, but it didn't mean I would just take what he was saying at face value. He had been delirious, close to death. He could have said a lot of things he didn't really mean. He might have just came with a mess of words for the sake of getting them off his chest. Perhaps he had been confused with the pain and the blood loss.

Or maybe he had been telling the truth. Because in all the time I had known him, I had never known Mauro to mis-speak. He picked his words carefully, chose every one to make sure they meant just what he intended them to. I couldn't imagine he would have let that slip in those vital final seconds that he had on this Earth, no matter how bad he might have felt.

I started going through his phone – his messages, his old calls, anything that I could use that might give me a hint as to what had been going on with him. But it wasn't until I opened his contacts that I found something that pointed to an answer.

One of the contacts was simply listed under *if I die.* My heart skipped a beat when I saw it. Had he known? Had he always known that this was a possibility, and that he needed to be ready for it? I hovered my finger over the call button, no idea if I should actually hit the button or if I should calm down a little first.

Shit. I didn't have a choice. I needed to get moving on this now. If Mauro was right, and Nikita really was about to bring war to my doorstep, I had to be ready and willing to fight him when he did. I clicked the call button and held the phone to my ear.

After a moment or two, someone answered.

"Mauro?"

"This isn't Mauro," I admitted at once. "This is Andreas. Andreas Salieri."

There was a pause on the other end of the line, the sound of breathing, like they were working out how to respond to that.

"Where's Mauro?"

"He's - he's dead," I told him. I couldn't believe I was saying it out loud, not really, but I had to come to terms with it at some point. He was gone, and I was out here on my own now. He was relying on me to do the right thing. I had to prove that he could.

The person on the call caught their breath, but it didn't seem to stun them. They must have been prepared for something like this. Given what Mauro did – if what he had told me had been true – then it had been coming for a long time.

"We need to meet," the person replied. It was a man, I was quite sure of that. The accent was throwing me, though. European? Not Italian, not Serbian – maybe French?

"When?" I asked. "Where?"

"I'll send you an address," he replied. "It's a couple of blocks from your apartment."

"How do you know where I—"

"Meet me there in three hours, sharp," he replied. "I'll speak to you soon."

And, with that, he hung up the phone.

Okay. Okay. I could do this. I needed to. It might not be easy, wrapping my head around everything that was being asked of me right now, but I could do it. I had to meet with this guy, even if I had no idea who he was or what his connection to Mauro might be. There was too much on the line, too much I couldn't let slip through my fingers. And with every second that ticked past, I was sure Nikita was drawing closer and closer, ready to take me out for good.

And Nadia – Nadia. I hadn't been able to stop thinking about her, her name thrumming at the back of my mind with every heartbeat. I needed to get her out of whatever mess she was trapped in right now. She might have left me, but I knew she wouldn't have done it unless she felt like she didn't have any other choice. This wasn't something she had done because she wanted to, it was something she had done because she felt she had to, and if I could change the circumstances, I might be able to get her back.

I organized some security to come with me to the address the mysterious caller had texted me. I knew it was dangerous, especially at a time like this, to head out somewhere with no knowledge of where I was going to end up, but that was the risk I was willing to take.

From this point on, I needed to throw myself at whatever I could to make it through this mess. Mauro had left me a trail of breadcrumbs, and I was going to follow them until the end of the line. No matter what. For his sake, for mine, for Nadia's - for the sake of my father's legacy, too. It was all on me now, and I was determined to see it through and prove I could do what needed to be done.

I had no idea how that caller had known where I lived, but true to his word, the address that he was sending me to was only a few blocks from my apartment. I was tailed by security, but I went in unarmed, knowing I had to play it cool. I had to make sure that whoever I was meeting with didn't have a reason to fear me, even if I wanted them to be scared right now.

The address led to a darkened bar, with blacked-out windows and a scruffy sign over the doorway. Not exactly the kind of place I was used to hanging out at, but I brushed it off. This wasn't about me. This was about doing the right thing, no matter how unsure I might have been about stepping over that threshold to find out what was waiting for me.

I approached the door, eyes darting back and forth to make sure nobody was following me. A slight rain had started to patter on the sidewalk, and the streets were quiet that day, as though the city was holding its breath. Waiting for something to happen.

I pushed the door to the bar open, and it groaned against its hinges as I stepped inside. The place smelled like booze and cheap cigarettes. The bartender, an older man with a scar running down one side of his cheek, looked up to see me enter, and then turned his attention back to buffing out the stains in the mottled bar in front of him.

I scanned the room, trying to find who I had come to meet. There weren't many people in the bar, so it wasn't exactly hard to make them out. A few older guys, sitting in the corner booths and sipping on booze, a younger couple in motorcycle leathers nearer the door, and then...

Over in the darkest corner of the bar, I saw him. The person I had spoken to on the phone. I knew it was him at once. The way he was looking at me, it couldn't be anyone else. I started towards his table, and he didn't move, not taking his eyes off of me as I drew closer.

In the dim light, I could make out a few details of his face. He was a little younger than Mauro – at least, I thought so. He seemed ageless, in a way, like a vampire, his face not creased but marked with the knowledge of years beyond those that he had lived. His eyes were sharp and gray, and he was wearing a well-made suit, tailored to fit his lean form.

"Andreas?" he asked me as I got close enough to hear him. I nodded. He jerked his head to the seat opposite him.

"Sit down," he ordered me. "We have a lot to talk about."

I did as I was told. He had a packet of cigarettes on the table, and he was rolling one between his fingers frantically, as though he was attempting to blow off steam. I knew how he felt. The tension was palpable, even as I tried to control my nerves. Did he have people watching us, too? Surely, he must have eyes on us right now, the same way I did. It was too dangerous to risk doing this without it.

"Mauro's dead?" he asked, and I nodded.

"I watched his body get wheeled out by the coroner just before I called you," I replied. "He was shot, by one of the Serbians, I believe."

"Shit," the man muttered, shaking his head. It was clear that was the last thing he'd wanted to hear.

He looked up at me. There was a coldness to him, but I knew in the line of work that Mauro had been in – and presumably this man, too – he had no choice but to keep it that way.

"I'm going to skip the pageantry," he told me quickly. "I'm Leo. I'm an FBI agent, I was working with Mauro on your and Nikita's cases."

I nodded. I still couldn't bring myself to believe that Mauro had really lied to me all this time, but as long as I kept getting this evidence that it was true, what other choice did I have?

"And, from this point forward, unless you do exactly what I tell you," he continued, narrowing his eyes at me. "Then you can consider yourself under arrest. You understand me?"

I nodded.

"I understand."

Chapter Fifteen

Nadia

AS I STOOD THERE, IN front of the mirror, in that beautiful white gown, all I could see was the ghost of my own form floating in front of me.

I was meant to be picking out a wedding dress – the dress that I was going to get married in, the one I would tie the knot to my soon-to-be husband while wearing. The gaggle of women around me, tugging at the fabric and nattering away to each other in Serbian, seemed excited, but there was a deep hollowness in my chest as I tried to make sense of what I was going to do.

"This one?" the shop assistant asked, sounding exhausted. I didn't blame her. We had already been through a bunch of dresses as it was, and she must have been wondering how long we were going to take to find one that we actually liked.

"No, no, can't you see in her face that she doesn't like it?" one of the women – a cousin of Nikita's, I was sure – exclaimed. "Get another one!"

The assistant backed off towards the other side of the shop, and I headed into the changing room to get out of this thing once more. I was already exhausted, and there was still so much left to do before the wedding the next day.

The moment the plane had touched down in New York, I had been whisked off by a gaggle of women related to Nikita to prepare for the wedding. It was happening tomorrow – so soon that I'd hardly have time to pull together the plan that I needed to – and there was a lot for them to work out before they sent me down that aisle.

I was dizzy, basically a jetlagged wreck from the flight, but the dozen or so women with me were making up for my lack of enthusiasm without a second thought. The assistant brought out another dress and handed it to me around the door, and I lingered for a moment before I put it on, enjoying the brief moment of quiet before I would have to go back out there and show myself off.

I couldn't believe I was doing this. I had always imagined planning my wedding to be a joyful affair, something I would linger over and indulge every second of, but instead, as I held the cream fabric to my chest, I wondered if there was still time for me to run.

I knew it was a stupid idea. My father was still in the city, and Nikita would take him out as soon as he found out I had fled. The last thing I needed was to put him in danger, after everything we had both done to get out of this mess. My chest ached when I thought of him, all that I had put him through, and all that might happen to him if I didn't go through with this awful wedding.

I climbed into the dress and looked at myself in the mirror. This one was beautiful. They all had been, really – Nikita had told the women to spare no expense, and that he would pay for anything they thought necessary. The dress, a slip that fell in soft waves down to my feet, with a sweetheart neckline encrusted with jewels, would have made me feel beautiful any other day.

But today, this day, knowing what it was going to be used for, I felt ill. I pulled back the curtain, and there were a few gasps and then some nods of agreement around the room. This was it – this was the dress. I simply had to get it.

I headed back behind the curtain to get dressed again, and caught a glimpse of myself in the mirror. This dress would likely be the last thing I ever wore. Because, when Nikita was dead, someone was going to have to pay for his passing – and I was certain they would work out that it was me who should pay the price.

It was the part of the plan I had been doing my best to ignore, the part where I would be held accountable for what happened. I had to be ready for what came next, for what happened when he was dead in our wedding bed. But I knew that anything would be better than allowing him to call me his wife. Anything would be better than going along with his twisted games and letting him think he had won me over.

I wasn't buying my wedding dress. I was buying my funeral outfit.

I stepped out once I was dressed, and let the women spirit me off to whatever they had planned for me next. I had no idea where I was being taken, but it didn't matter, not really. All that mattered was that I kept up the façade as best I could, and made sure everyone believed I wanted to marry Nikita.

But surely, they must have been able to see through me. They must have been able to spot the emptiness in my heart, the deadness behind my eyes. Maybe none of them cared – they just wanted Nikita married off, and they didn't care what it took to make that happen. I hated that I had to go along with it, but at least they weren't trying to get me to speak about how thrilled I was with all of this.

I just needed to get the fuck through today, and it would all be behind me. They dragged me to a spa next, where I got my hair cut and my nails done. I couldn't remember the last time I had been able to indulge myself with stuff as lovely as this, and I wished I could have enjoyed it. All I could think about was that this was for him, for Nikita, and I loathed every second of it, wished I could have turned myself into a monster to keep him away.

But that wouldn't have stopped him. He had already decided he was going to have a piece of me, no matter what, and nothing I could have tried would have changed his mind on that. No matter how grotesque I was, no matter how disgusting I tried to make myself, I knew that he would find some way to pull me back into his web and get me to be his bride.

I looked down at my pearly-pink nails. They would have been pretty, in any other circumstance, but knowing that all of this was for him made me feel sick. I hated the thought of prettifying myself just for him to get his hands on; not that I had much choice, but still. I wanted to scrub myself of all of it, make it so he didn't get to see me this way.

The women I was with, I felt bad for them. Because they were all so excited about what was to come, and here I was, acting as though the world was about to be ripped out from underneath me. They tried to make conversation, but my answers were brief and boring. I had nothing to say. I just wanted this to be over.

But when it was over... I doubted I would be around to see it. Would these women turn on me, too? For all their sweetness now, if they had even the barest inkling that I had been the one to take out Nikita, I was sure they would tear me apart with their bare hands. Every Serbian in the city would turn on me, the last safe haven I had pulled out from underneath me, once and for all.

By the time we were done at the spa, I was spent. All of this was meant to be relaxing and rejuvenating, but, in truth, it made me feel even more empty and more hopeless than before. I couldn't believe I was going through with this. I couldn't believe that I would allow myself, for an instant, to be pulled into this nightmare. But what choice had Nikita given me? He had made it so I had no way out except to marry him, to let him call me his wife.

I prayed I would be able to finish him off before he got me to bed. The thought of his awful hands on me made my stomach turn, and I wasn't sure I would be able to fake it long enough to convince him of anything. Would he even care? He clearly didn't give a damn that I barely wanted this marriage, and I had no doubt that he would be willing to utterly overlook my lack of interest in him physically, too.

The women finally let me go once our trip to the spa was done, and I told them that I needed time to rest; the wedding was early tomorrow, and I wanted to be ready for it. One of them, Lina, pulled me into her arms for an excited hug.

"It's going to be the most wonderful day," she murmured to me. I tried to keep the smile on my face. Just a few more hours of convincing everyone, and it would all be over. I would finally be free.

But there was something I needed to do before I could rest easy tonight, and that was to speak to my father. I was sure he was already trying to work out what was going on, how I had agreed to this wedding as quickly as I had, and I wanted to put his mind at ease.

He was back at our apartment, the one next to the store, and I caught a cab down there and paused outside the entrance. There was so much memory wrapped up in this place, and I was about to leave it all behind for good. I had no idea how I would be able to just leave it, but I had to. I had to accept that this place wasn't for me anymore, that I needed to move on and accept what was to come. If it protected my father, the life that he had made for himself here, then it would be worth it.

It would be worth it.

I headed up to the apartment and unlocked the door to find him dozing on the couch; his eyes sprang open as soon as he heard me, and he smiled.

"Nadia," he murmured, and he rose to his feet to pull me into a warm hug. I closed my eyes and hugged him back, holding him close; I never wanted this to end, never wanted to let him go. But when I pulled back, he must have been able to see how serious I was, because his face darkened with fear.

"What is it?" he asked. "What are you doing here? Shouldn't you be getting ready for the wedding?"

"I already have," I promised him. "I – I need to talk to you, Dad. Now. I don't know if I'll have time tomorrow, before everything happens."

"The wedding, you mean?" he asked, and I nodded.

"Yeah, of course, the wedding," I replied. Honestly, just thinking about it made me want to shudder in disgust. I hated feeling this way, feeling like I had to go through with everything Nikita demanded from me. At least it wouldn't be for long. Not if I had anything to do with it.

"Tomorrow, I'm going to send a car down here for you," I told him. "Early in the morning. It's going to take you somewhere – well, somewhere safe. Somewhere far away from here, okay?"

"What are you talking about?" he asked, utterly confused. "You – I'm going to be at the wedding, of course I am, where else would I be?"

"I can't answer those questions right now," I told him, my voice catching at the back of my throat. "I want to, I do, but it's safer for you not to know. Safer for both of us."

He shook his head.

"I'm not missing out on this," he replied. "Not the day I've been waiting for my whole life."

"You really waited your whole life for me to marry a man like Nikita?" I asked him, and his face fell.

"I... Nadia, what are you trying to say?"

"It doesn't matter," I replied urgently. I was sure Nikita had someone keeping an eye on me right now, and I had no doubt that he would do what he could to try to keep me away from my father. It must have crossed his mind that I might attempt something to take him down.

"I just need you to listen to me and to trust me," I continued, as calmly as I could. "Do you understand?"

He nodded.

"I trust you, Nadia," he murmured. "I trust you more than anyone in the world."

"Good," I replied. "I need you to get into that car when it comes tomorrow morning, and get as far from the city as you can, you understand?"

He nodded. He didn't say anything.

"Thank you," I replied. He put his arms around me, pulled me into a tight hug – I could feel the tears pricking my eyes, and I tried my best to ignore them. This was all too much for me to take on right now. I had too much on my mind to handle his pain too, but at the same time, I didn't want to let go of him. I wanted to hold on to him for the rest of my life, make it so nothing could pull us apart.

"Can you tell me what you're going to do?" he asked, and I shook my head. The less he knew, the better. The safer he would be. I was doing all this for him, to make sure that he remained safe, and I wasn't going to compromise that by sharing my vague plan with him.

"I'm sorry," I murmured to him. "And I'm - I'm sorry I couldn't protect you myself."

"That's my job," my father replied, a small smile on his face. I felt the tears begin to rise, but I swallowed them back down again. If this was the last chance I was going to have to be with him, I didn't want to spend it weeping over everything we had lost.

So, instead, I hugged him again, squeezing him close enough that I was sure we would never be pulled apart. I closed my eyes, and let the feeling of my father soothe me into believing I was doing the right thing.

And give me the strength to do what needed to be done tomorrow. Nikita would get what he deserved, and my father would be safe. That was all that mattered to me.

Chapter Sixteen

Andreas

LEO SAT OPPOSITE ME, rolling the unlit cigarette between his fingers, waiting for me to respond.

"Under arrest?" I asked, and he nodded.

"That's the best I can offer," he replied. "That doesn't involve sticking you in the back of a van and taking you away right now."

I winced. I knew I had been taking a risk coming out here, but this was a bigger one than I had been prepared for. I couldn't go to prison, not now – there was too much on the line, too many pieces in the air to even think about it.

"So why aren't you doing that?" I asked.

"Because we need you to help us stop Nikita," Leo explained. "Mauro's led me to believe that you're trustworthy, at least as far as your rivalry with the Serbians is concerned. And I need you to prove that to me, right now."

"Doing what?" I asked, shaking my head. I had no idea what he was going to ask of me. But I had to be willing to play along with them. It was strange to think of Mauro working with these people, making it so they knew everything about me, but I had to accept it was the truth. There was no way they could have made this up.

"Okay, let me tell you what we have on the Nikita situation," he told me, leaning back in his seat. He glanced around us, making sure that nobody was listening in, before he continued.

"He's planning to marry Nadia tomorrow," he explained, and I had to clench my fist under the table to keep from reacting. I already knew that, but it didn't make it any easier to hear it coming out of his mouth. Nikita really thought that he could just take Nadia from me, as though it was that easy? He had another fucking thing coming.

"But, in truth, he's going to use it to start an all-out war with you and your cohorts," Leo continued. "Now, that's the last thing we want. It's hard enough to keep you both out of trouble without more reason for you to fight than ever."

"I don't get it," I replied, shaking my head. "We're - how is him getting married to Nadia going to lead to a war?"

"Because he's not going to let her make it out of their reception," he replied. "They're going to have their first dance, and he's going to have someone pick her off before she can so much as cut the cake."

My eyes widened and my stomach dropped.

"What the fuck are you talking about?" I demanded. The thought of Nadia in some beautiful gown, being taken out by some bastard on her wedding day stuck in my brain at once, lodging itself inside in that dangerous, frightening way that only losing someone you loved could.

"He's setting it up to make it look as though you're the one who killed her," Leo explained. "He's going to be weeping over her body and then he's going to declare war on you and your people. What better reason to fight than over his wife?"

"He's going to kill her," I muttered, and I felt the rage rise inside of me before I could get hold of it. I knew I needed to stay calm, hear Leo out, but this was more than I could take. How could he do something like that? It was bad enough that he seemed to think he had any claim over Nadia at all, but this was something else entirely.

I was going to stop it before it so much as got started.

"Not if we can help it," Leo replied. "If he does, and if he gets that story out there – the city's going to be on fire by the end of the night. People you thought you could trust will turn on you, if they believe his story, and they're going to. They won't believe that he could have killed his own wife just to push this narrative further forward, and they're going to do whatever they can to destroy you."

I tried to wrap my head around it. The plan was a good one, honestly. If I could look at it with a little clarity, I could see that Nikita would get everything that he wanted from selling this story, no matter how much I hated the mere thought of it. He could convince the world that I was a monster willing to murder a young bride on the day of her wedding to get what I wanted, and he could pull in everyone around him to make sure I got what was coming to me.

But I couldn't let that happen. I hardly cared about what would happen to me, but the thought of losing Nadia – no. Not a fucking chance in hell. I wasn't going to let Nikita take her from me, from the world at large. She deserved better than that. She had been through enough. I wasn't going to let her life end that way, with that indignity, as part of some scheme an evil man had come up with to win a game that he had been playing all his life.

"How do you know all this?" I asked him, narrowing my eyes.

"Because Mauro's the one who helped put this all in place," Leo replied.

"What the hell are you talking about?"

"He's the one who arranged for Nikita and Nadia to come together," he explained. I shook my head.

"He would never have done that—"

"There's a lot you don't know about Mauro, trust me," Leo cut me off. "A lot that you'll probably never know. But he was working with the Serbians behind your back. It was his way of making sure we could keep control of both ends of this. We didn't want to lose our grip on you or on Nikita, but once Mauro realized things were reaching a boiling point, he decided that we needed to take Nikita out."

"Why not me?" I asked, hollowly. "Why wouldn't Mauro just get rid of me, if I'm that much of a problem?"

"I think he grew fond of you, despite the circumstances of your meeting," Leo replied, grimly. "And he knows we have a better chance of controlling the Italians rather than the Serbians. Nikita – well, he's a loose cannon. We have no way to know what he's planning on doing at any given time, and we're not willing to take that risk."

"So you set Nadia up with him... for what?" I asked.

"As a distraction," Leo replied. "If he's focused on the wedding, then we have the chance to take out the Serbians and destabilize their organization."

"Mauro set Nadia up to be killed by Nikita?" I asked, shaking my head. He might have been lying to me about some things, but surely he wouldn't have put an innocent girl in so much danger.

"The intention was never to let her be taken out by him," Leo assured me. "We planned to lure them back to New York so we had a fix on Nikita, and kill him the night before the wedding was due to happen."

"Tonight?"

"That was the plan."

"And what is it now?"

He sighed.

"Some things have... changed, compared to how we wanted them to be," he admitted. "We intended to take Nikita out and rescue Nadia, let her talk about what she's been through in the hopes of changing the public perception of Nikita once and for all. But he's got her right where he wants her, and I'm not convinced we can go through with the assassination and get her out in one piece."

"So what do we do now?" I demanded.

"That's where you come in," he explained, pointing the cigarette in my direction. "We need you to get Nadia out of there. We can't risk her going through with the wedding. If she does, Nikita will have the opportunity to pull the trigger on his plan – literally. If she ends up dead, then we have no control over any of this anymore, and we can't risk that happening."

"And what are you asking me to do?" I pressed him. I knew that it must be galling for a man like him to have to deal with someone like me, but that's how I knew it had to be serious. There was no way they would have even entertained pulling me into this unless they had a damn good reason to. This was as important as they came, and I would do anything to make sure I didn't lose Nadia just because of some plan Mauro had come up with behind my back.

"I'm asking you to get in there and steal your girlfriend," he replied, a smile spreading over his face. "You leave everything else to us."

He lifted the cigarette to his lips and lit it. It was utterly illegal to smoke indoors, but I got the feeling he didn't care much about that. This was a man who was used to having everything his own way, and he wasn't going to let anything get in the way of that.

I nodded. My mind was racing as I tried to piece together my plan. I knew that I had to act fast, that I had to make sure I pulled this off – if Nadia got hurt, or worse, I would never come close to forgiving my-self. I had to pull a plan out of my ass that would ensure she stayed safe, no matter how tough it might be, no matter how hard I was pressed against the clock right now.

The smoke from his cigarette curled around his face, and he eyed me. I could tell he didn't trust me, certainly not after what had hap-pened to Mauro, and maybe I couldn't blame him for that. This man wanted to be able to put his faith in me, but I was still a villain in his eyes – the lesser of two evils, but not by a whole lot.

"You're not going to let me down on this, are you?" he asked me bluntly. I shook my head.

"You know I won't," I replied. I meant it. No matter how much I might be freaking out, I had to come through with this, more than I had ever come through with anything before. Yes, Mauro was gone, but that didn't mean I couldn't handle myself. When it came to Nadia, I would find the strength that I needed to see it through.

Because if I didn't - then she would be stuck with Nikita for the rest of her short life. And there was no way in fucking hell I would let that piece of shit get anywhere close to the woman I loved. The fact that he had convinced her to agree to this wedding in the first place was bad enough, but on top of that, for him to use her for this twisted plan... he had no idea what was coming his way.

I watched Leo as he smoked his cigarette and wondered if I could trust him. I was just learning about Mauro's secret double-life, and I didn't know if I could believe everything that came out of Leo's mouth. But I didn't have a choice. He was the closest thing to an ally that I had left in the world right now, and I had to work with what I was being given.

The smell of the tobacco filled the air around me, and I narrowed my eyes against the smoke. Whatever it took, I was going to see this through. I was going to get Nadia out.

And I was going to keep her from spending another fucking minute with the nightmare that was Nikita.

Chapter Seventeen

Nadia

I PERCHED ON THE EDGE of the bed, staring into space. I had no idea how to feel right now, and honestly, I wasn't sure I would be able to sleep tonight.

Even though I was exhausted from the day behind me, my mind was too wired to just lay back and get some rest. How could I? I knew that what the next day would bring would change everything, one way or another, and I needed it to be over with already.

I had managed to borrow a phone from one of the girls I had been with that day, so I could organize a car to pick up my father and get him out of the city. He was the main thing on my mind right now, I needed to know he would be safe and stay far from here.

I had to pray that nobody would notice that he wasn't at the wedding. If they did – shit, the whole plan could go to hell right then and there. Nikita would know I didn't want to do anything without my dad there, and the only reason I would have tried to get him out of the city was because I didn't intend on sticking around much longer myself.

But then – there were going to be so many people there, the crowds so intense, I had to hope nobody would pay much attention to him not turning up. By the time that the ceremony started, he could be a hundred miles out of New York, and hopefully nobody would think to go looking for him. He had nothing to do with this, and I was going to keep it that way – give him as much freedom as I could from the nightmare I was going to bring down on my own head.

Speaking of. I had been going back and forth all day, trying to work out how best to carry out my plan. I wanted to use poison to off Nikita, certain that it would give me the distance from him I needed to make this work, but it wasn't so easy to find any. I was being followed around most of the day by those women who had basically been assigned to get me ready for marriage, and I had no way to slip off and find something I could use to take out the man I was supposed to be pledging my life to the next day.

So I would have to do it with my bare hands. Which sounded ridiculous, even to me – I was way weaker than Nikita, even if I got the jump on him and landed it with the element of surprise. He would take me out in no time, and when he did he would kill me.

I was sure of it. I had been thinking about it all night long, and it was the only way I could see it going down. He wasn't going to take any kind of insubordination. He would wipe me off the face of the earth the moment I did anything that didn't fit with his fantasy for me, and an attack would be just that.

But I had to try. I couldn't marry him and just play along with his image of me as the doting wife. I needed him to know I wasn't going to give in the way everyone around him always had, I was better than that – I was stronger than that. Even if I couldn't go through with the murder, I could, at least, make it so he didn't have me right where he wanted me.

I would do it on the wedding night. When he least expected it. I had tried to convince him as best I could that I would be willing to give myself to him once and for all when our wedding night came, but in truth, I was planning something far darker. Maybe because the thought of it, of him touching me and trying to kiss me, made me want to vomit, made me want to claw my skin from my body just to be sure that he didn't have a chance to touch it.

He didn't care about it, though. Didn't care that I hated him. He just cared that he had me where he wanted me. This was a man who was used to having everything his own way, no matter the feelings of the people around him on the matter – he was willing to shit on everyone close to him, as long as it meant he got the life he wanted.

Which was why he was so miserably alone in the first place. It seemed obvious to me, but I doubted he would admit it, even to himself. He would never be able to say it out loud, tell himself that he was the problem. Much as he liked to frame himself as this tolerant guy who wanted the best for his community, he was a control-freak, a monster who needed every tiny detail to run the way he wanted it to or he would lose his fucking mind.

I wasn't going to let him have me. Yes, I would go through with the wedding, if only because it would give my father more time to get out of the city and to safety. But as soon as we were alone together, as soon as I got the chance, I was going to strike, and he was going to understand that he had never had me the way he thought he did.

It was the only thing giving me any peace on this long night ahead of me. I knew I wouldn't see another, and I was doing my best to come to terms with that. My heart pounded in my chest as I tried to imagine it, the anger in his eyes when he realized I had turned on him. I knew what he was capable of, I knew how he would act if he didn't get what he wanted, but the satisfaction of knowing that I had beaten him at his own game would be all I needed to get me through this in one piece.

I could handle it. I could accept my fate. As long as I knew my father was safe, I'd know I had done the right thing, and I could go into the next day happy with the choices I had made.

I needed to rest if I was going to be able to stand on my own two feet for the ceremony tomorrow, but honestly, my body wasn't going to give me that. I was exhausted from putting on the game face that I had for the girls I had spent the whole day with; I almost felt bad for lying to them, letting them think I was happy with all of this when I wished that I could have found any way out of it. But they would never have accepted my misery. No doubt more than a couple of them had hoped that they would see themselves in my place, marrying a man as powerful as Nikita, and if I had expressed even the slightest bit of doubt, they wouldn't have waited to show me their disdain.

I looked down at the pretty pink on my freshly-manicured nails; this was what I would be buried in. It was hard to imagine it, really. I had always thought I'd have more time, that there would come a point in my life where I would be able to pursue the things that really made me happy again, like dance, but it was clear I wasn't going to have that chance. I had to accept it. This was a noble way to go out, keeping my family safe and denying that evil man the chance to call me his. Better to be in the ground than wearing a ring that bound me to someone like Nikita, I was sure of it.

My mind drifted to Andreas, for what had to be the hundredth time that day. I wished I could speak to him, just one more time before I was gone. I'd tell him I never wanted to do this with Nikita. I was sure he could already have guessed it, but I wanted to look him in the eyes and make sure he understood that my feelings for him had been real in a way that the ones I had for Nikita never would be. I would have walked down the aisle for him, but for Nikita, it was just something I had to do. Something I had no choice but to go through with.

I had thought of calling him, but I was sure it would raise some alarms, and I didn't want to drag him back into this and get him hurt in the process. Mauro had told me to let go of Andreas, and I needed to accept it was over between us. It had been as soon as I had left New York, no matter how much I wished I could have stayed with him. He was a man leading his own empire, and if he was going to have a woman by his side, then she needed to be solidly there, not drifting in and out the way I had been.

I hoped he would find that woman, I really did. It pained me to think of him with someone else, but it would be unfair of me to expect him to sit around, mooning for me for the rest of his life. Our connection had been intense, and I knew I would never be able to replace it or even replicate it with anyone else, but I was sure he would be able to find women who would make him feel that way again.

The way Nikita had been talking to me about him, it sounded like he might already have done just that. I was trying not to imagine him with anyone else. If this was my last night on Earth, then the least I could do was not torture myself with the thought of him with someone else. I just hoped he was happy, hoped that he didn't know what I was doing with Nikita and that he would never have to find out why I had left him.

I lay down on the bed and stared at the ceiling. My brain was buzzing with everything that was about to happen, no way was I going to be able to sleep, but I had to try. I needed all my strength if I was going to stand a chance against Nikita the next day. If I was going to be able to convince anyone for a damn second that I wanted to go through with any of this.

I could imagine the way he would look at me at the altar, and the thought of his cruel face trying to contain any measure of emotion seemed almost funny. I would have to bite back the laughter when I was there in front of him, that was for sure.

There was a knock at the door, and I snapped upright. Had one of the women come back? Maybe the girl, looking for her phone? I honestly didn't have the energy to handle them right now.

"I'm trying to sleep!" I hissed into the darkness. I was staying in one of Nikita's apartments in the city, a place I had demanded for myself so I would be able to have some peace on my last night, but there were guards scattering the corridors.

"Let me in."

The voice that came back was not one that belonged to a woman – it was deep, masculine, and my heart skipped several beats inside my chest.

Nikita. There was nobody else it could be. He was here to take what he wanted from me, refusing to wait for our wedding night.

He had another fucking thing coming. I looked around the room quickly, trying to find something I could use to make my attack. If he wanted our wedding night early, then I would give it to him – just not in the way he expected. My eyes fell on a small letter-opener by the window, glinting in the darkness. I doubted it was very strong, but I didn't have a whole lot to go on right now. I needed to take the chance that I had.

I grabbed the small knife and started on my way to the door, my blood rushing to my head. Could I really do this? I didn't have a choice. When I answered this door with a knife, Nikita would know what my plans were. He wouldn't wait to show me what he thought of them.

I paused next to the door. Shit. My palms were sweating. I wasn't sure I could go through with this. Was I a killer? I had never thought I would be, but I wasn't certain I had much of a choice any longer. I had to do this. I had to. It was for the good of my family. I closed my eyes, and brought to mind my mother's face – all that she had done for me, all that she had sacrificed to make sure that I was okay. This was for her, to save the man she loved. The very least I could do.

I put my hand on the door and squeezed the knob for a moment. This was my last chance to back out, my last chance to hold back and live my life as Nikita's unwilling bride. My last chance to stop myself before this went any further...

Fuck it. There was no way I was going to let him win. I would fight this man till my dying breath if that's what it took. I felt the pressure of the blade in my hand, and pulled open the door, promising myself that I would fight to the death if that's what I needed to do—

But it wasn't Nikita standing there waiting for me. Of course it wasn't. No, it was the only man I'd been dreaming of this entire time, standing before me like a mirage, like a magic trick I had conjured from the air.

"Andreas?" I gasped. And without a second thought, I pulled him over the threshold, burying my face in his neck, and held him close enough that I was sure we would never be able to be pulled apart again.

Chapter Eighteen

Andreas

AS I HELD HER IN MY arms, for a moment, I wondered if I should have known better than to come here.

I knew it was dangerous. I knew that we could be busted at any moment. But here, now, with her so close to me, none of it seemed to matter. None of it could. Nadia was here, in my arms, where she belonged.

I pulled back to plant my lips against hers, needing to taste her, to feel her so close to me again. Nothing mattered, nothing could, but the feeling of us coming together like this. She kissed me back, and it felt like a dream – something out of a fantasy that I had never been able to live out before, being in love. Being with a woman who loved me just as much back.

She clasped my face in her hands and gazed into my eyes as though making sure I was really there. I knew how she felt – it almost seemed impossible, as though we didn't stand a chance of this being real. But, as I gazed at her, took in all the details on her perfect face, I knew she was here. That we were here, together – and nothing else in the damn world mattered other than that.

I brushed my nose against hers, and she smiled.

"I can't believe it," she murmured. "You're here. You're... you're actually here."

"You really thought you were going to get rid of me that easily?" I asked her as I pushed the door shut behind me. Even though I was well-aware that we working against the clock here, I wanted to take a moment to show her how much I had missed her. If I could have carried her to that bed and proved it to her properly, I would have, but I knew I had to hold back, at least for now. At least until we were out of here.

"Thought I might," she joked back, and I chuckled. Even in the midst of the chaos that was unfolding around us, she still knew how to make me laugh, and I couldn't think of anything better than that. The reason I had come here, because our connection ran deeper than just the physical – we knew that we shared something profound, and nothing was going to get in the way of us enjoying it.

"We need to get out of here," I told her urgently, and she shook her head.

"How the hell are we going to do that?"

I pulled the bag that I had draped over my shoulder around to my chest, and pulled out the stuff I had managed to grab before I had come out here. It might not have been a lot, but it was something – the best that I could come up with on short notice.

I handed her a men's shirt and blazer, along with the smallest pair of men's pants that I had been able to dig out - I was sure that they would still swamp her, but it was the best I could do right now. And then, I pressed some scissors into her hand as well.

"What's this for?" she asked, furrowing her brow. I took a deep breath, knowing that she wasn't going to be happy with what I said next.

"You need to cut your hair off," I explained. "I'm going to disguise you as a waiter, one of the staff for the wedding – it's the best chance we have of getting out of here in one piece."

Her eyes flickered with doubt for a second, but it was soon replaced with sureness. She tensed her fingers around the scissors, then handed them to me.

"Here, take these," she told me, as she pulled her hair into a ponytail. I was surprised that she wasn't putting up more of a fight right now, but she likely knew as well as I did that we were going to have to move fast if we were going to get through all of this in one piece. I had no idea what the stakes were for her, no idea if she had any clue what Nikita had planned for her, but she was still treating this as a matter of life and death.

"Cut here," she told me, pointing to the base of her ponytail. I didn't need to be told twice. Every second that we were here was another second that someone could walk in and find us, and there was no way that I was going to let anything stop me getting her out of here alive.

I snipped her ponytail, cutting it off as quickly and as neatly as I could. I knew it wasn't going to be easy for her, but she didn't even flinch – she looked at her reflection in the window as she pulled away her ponytail in her hand, her eyes not giving away any sadness.

"I need to change," she told me, as she stuffed the ponytail down the side of the bed – good plan, since she knew that anyone who came in here looking for her after she fled would be searching for any small detail that they could to find out where she had run to. She clasped the clothes to her chest and headed for the bathroom. She could have stripped in front of me, but I knew that would have made it all too easy to get distracted, and both of us needed to keep our heads in the game right now.

I glanced back and forth as I listened to her changing, wondering how long we had before someone spotted something going on. Surely, people would be keeping an eye on her in this room, making sure that she didn't try to make a break for it. Or perhaps Nikita was already certain he had her where he wanted her. Did he realize she was looking for the first way out that she could find? I almost wanted to tell him, but I knew we couldn't blow it open like this, not so close to getting out in one piece.

When Nadia emerged, she looked totally different – she had done her best to tighten and fit the clothes to her body, and, with her newly-short hair slicked back, she could have passed for a member of staff. I took her hand and pulled her towards the door. She hesitated.

"I – I don't know if I can do this," she admitted, her eyes wide with fear. "My father—"

"Your father's going to be fine," I swore to her. "But right now, we need to get you out of here. Okay?"

"Okay," she replied, with a nod, even though she still didn't sound sure. I knew it was going to take her a while to be certain of what she was doing, but I would take care of her. I would make sure she had no reason to doubt this, or any choice that she made with me. We were going to get her out of here, and then, we were going to take Nikita down any way we could.

I pushed open the door, glanced back and forth, and found the place empty. Okay. We just needed to get to the bottom of the stairs, out the door, and there was a car waiting just down the street to whisk us away from here, thank goodness. I could feel my heart thumping in my chest as she followed close behind me, her breath coming hard and fast. I knew she was scared, but I would do anything I could to make sure she got out alive. She had to trust me. And I knew I had to earn it.

We headed along the corridor to the top of the stairs, where one of the guards was slumped over – I'd taken him out on the way up, shutting him down for at least the night, and Nadia looked at him fearfully.

"He's not going to stop us," I promised her quietly. "Come on, we have to keep moving."

We arrived at the top of the stairs, and I peered down into the darkness to make sure that there was nobody there waiting for us. There didn't seem to be. If we just got outside, we would be in the clear, and we were so close to that already. Just a few more steps, and I would get her out of this place. I could almost smell the cool city air beyond the door, and I knew she could, too. We were so close...

We took the stairs two at a time, and I wished that I could clasp on to her hand as we went, but I knew that might blow our cover. As soon as we were out of here, we would be able to do anything we wanted. We just had to hold out for a little while longer—

"Hey, hold up!"

A voice cut through the dimly-lit corridor that led to the front door, and I froze on the spot. Shit. Someone had seen us. I had no clue who it was, who might have been talking around these corridors this late at night and what they might have been looking for, but we had to think fast.

"Hey," I called back, trying to sound as casual as possible. "You okay, dude?"

"What are you doing here?" the voice continued, and a man emerged from the shadows beyond us to attach himself to it. He was shaven-headed, his eyes squinting at me in the half-darkness. Nadia drew back a little behind me, knowing that if anything was going to tip him off, it would be her.

"We were sent down by Nikita to pick up some clothes for tomorrow," I replied, as smoothly as I could. I had already considered the possibility of being caught out by someone down here, and I figured that the best way to deal with it would be to pretend we were staff. She could almost pass as some random waiter, with her new short hair and men's clothes, and I had to hope that this guy didn't bother to look too closely at the two of us right now.

"What are you picking up?" he asked, tilting his chin up as he continued to eye me.

"We're picking up an outfit for the bride to change into after the wedding," I explained, and I raised my eyebrows at him. "Something that Nikita is *very* much looking forward to. I don't think he'd be happy to hear that anyone had gotten in the way of that."

The man paused for a moment, and for a second, I thought that he was going to argue with me – but instead, he shrugged, clearly thinking better of it than to argue about something Nikita apparently wanted so badly.

"All right," he muttered. "Well. Make it quick. I don't want people coming in and out of here all night."

"We're leaving now," I assured him, and Nadia strode over to the door. The man glanced at her, and I held my breath, waiting for him to click that this was the woman he was meant to be keeping an eye on – but he didn't seem to notice anything. She didn't wait, pushing the door open and waiting for me to join her.

As soon as we were out on to the street, I hustled her towards the van I had waiting for us. I glanced behind me, to see the man who had been talking to us watching as we headed for it.

"What if he sends someone after the van to find us?" she breathed. Her voice sounded like it had caught in the back of her throat, and I knew she had every reason to be scared right now.

"He can't," I assured her. "We have a few other vehicles waiting for us. This is just the first one."

She nodded, and I pulled open the back of the van and guided her inside. I was so relieved that she was here with me, I almost couldn't put it into words. I had really believed, for a long while there, that she was gone from my life, that we might never get a chance to see each other again. Now that she was here, with me, where she belonged, all of that seemed to just fall away like it was nothing. Her closeness reminded me why I had done all of this in the first place – that I would have done it all again if that's what it took, because I was always going to find a way back to her.

I was always going to find a way to keep her close to me.

I pulled her close in the back of the van, as it pulled away from where she had been held. The driver was one of my own men, and he knew where we were going. There were a few more stop-offs waiting for us before we got to the town car that would whisk us out of the city, but the hard part was over now. I had gotten her out of that building, and I couldn't think of much more in the world that mattered than that.

"Are you okay?" I murmured to her, and she nodded.

"I will be," she replied. "I – I thought I was going to have to marry that piece of shit..."

"I would never have let it happen," I promised her. She grinned at me, looking at me sideways.

"You came there even though you didn't know what I thought," she remarked. "What if I'd wanted to spend the rest of my life with that guy? Would that have stopped you?"

"It would have made me question the hell out of your taste," I quipped back. "But it wouldn't have stopped me."

She leaned her head on my shoulder and closed her eyes.

"I'm so glad you came back for me," she murmured. "I thought I would never see you again."

I wrapped my arms around her, too exhausted to think of much more to say to her than that. The fact that she was here and she was with me seemed to be all I could focus on right now. As long as we had each other, we would make it through this whole mess, I was sure of it. We just needed to keep the wheels turning underneath us, and we would survive. Survive together.

The van stopped at a drop-off point just outside of the city, and I ushered Nadia to our next vehicle, a small minibus that would give us plenty of space to hide. She didn't let go of my hand the entire time, her eyes fixed to the window as the city sped by outside, and I watched her carefully. I knew she had to be going through a lot right now, but I wanted her to know that she would be able to trust me through all of it. I was going to get her, and her father, out of here totally and utterly safe, and nothing was going to get in the way of that. I loved her, and I was going to ensure that she was okay, no matter how much it took out of me.

The bus stopped another half-hour or so outside of the city, pulling to a halt next to a small, sleek black car; I recognized the driver in the front seat as the one Leo had introduced me to before all of this had started, and I opened the door for Nadia and helped her in.

"Is this the last one?" she asked, and I nodded.

"Just one more, and then we'll get to the safe house in New Jersey."

She nodded, looking relieved. I knew she had been through it these last few weeks, and the last couple of hours in particular, but now that she was here, she was safe. I needed her to believe that.

I squeezed her hand from the other side of the back seat, and she looked up at me as though she could hardly believe that this was really happening.

"You came back for me," she murmured, and I nodded.

"I always will," I promised her. "You have nothing to worry about. I'm always going to come back for you."

That seemed enough to sate her for the time being; she returned her gaze to the window once more and watched the scenery whipping by outside, a promise that we were leaving far behind us anything and everything we could to get away. She never had to worry about Nikita again. I was here for her, and I would always get her out – always find a way for her to escape, no matter how hard it might be.

And maybe, by now, she was starting to believe it. Even though it must have been hard – even though she must still have been scared. I was going to get her out, no matter what, and soon, we would be able to talk about it all properly.

She skimmed a hand over her newly short hair, and waited for us to arrive wherever we were going.

Chapter Nineteen

Nadia

AS I STEPPED OUT OF the car at last, I let out a sigh of relief. I was out of there.

At least, for now.

"You okay?" Andreas asked as he draped an arm around my shoulders. I still couldn't believe that he had really done that, staged such a dramatic break-out just to make sure I escaped Nikita's grasp. I had been so ready to do whatever it took to make sure that I took Nikita out, but Andreas had saved me the weight of it.

"I think so," I murmured. "I – what about my father? I was going to send a car for him tomorrow, but I—"

"We've already gotten him out," Andreas assured me. "He's heading to one of our safehouses in Vancouver right now. He's going to hide out there for a while, with all of our security and everything – he couldn't be anywhere safer."

I nodded, still feeling a little wobbly. I wished I could have seen my father in person, but that would come when the time was right, and clearly, that wasn't now. I needed him to know that I was okay, too, that both of us had somehow managed to make it out alive, despite everything that had happened – despite the mess that had unfolded of our lives, we would survive it, the way we always had.

I could feel the tears starting to rise inside of me, the stress and the shock of everything starting to catch up with me at last, as Andreas led me inside the New Jersey safehouse that we would be staying in for the foreseeable future. It wasn't much, just a small place with about a dozen armed guards outside, but it felt like a damn holiday resort compared to where I had been before. Stuck in that room, counting down the seconds until I had to marry a man I hated, anywhere would have been a relief in comparison. But here? With Andreas? It was more than I had imagined possible, and I would never stop being grateful for it.

"Come on, you need to get some rest," Andreas told me, as he guided me up the stairs towards a bedroom waiting for me at the top. I was so grateful for him, I didn't even know how to put it into words. I wished I could tell him, in no uncertain terms, that I was beyond grateful for everything that he had done, but I didn't have the energy to think of the right way to do it.

I headed to the small ensuite bathroom attached to our bedroom, and looked at myself in the mirror. It was the first time I had laid eyes on myself since I had cut all my hair off, and yeah, it was a shock. I reached up to run my fingers through my new cropped mop, and I wondered how long it would take to grow it all back again.

Maybe it was better like this. Maybe it was easier on me to just leave all that behind, some version of myself that had existed before all of this had happened. The thought of it energized something in me. That long hair had been attached to the woman who had been stuck about to marry someone she hated just to protect her family – but now, here, in all of this, I could be okay. I could leave it all behind. I could lop it off and not care a bit about it.

There was a robe hanging over the back of the door, and I changed out of the ill-fitting clothes Andreas had brought for me and slipped into a shower. I tipped my head back as the cool water rushed over my face, and I couldn't help but smile. It was as though all the weight that I had been lugging around with me had finally started to lift, and I knew I could move on. My father was safe. I was with Andreas. I couldn't think of much more in the world that mattered than that.

I washed off the stress of everything that had happened, and slipped that robe over my shoulders, wrapping it around me before I emerged into the bedroom once more. Andreas was sitting on the edge of the bed, and he grinned as soon as he saw me.

"You look good with that short hair, you know," he remarked, and I ran my fingers through it.

"It could use a little attention from an actual hairdresser," I replied. "But yeah. I don't mind it as much as I thought I would."

"You're saying that you don't think I already did a perfect job?" he asked, playing at being insulted, and I laughed as I slipped down on to the bed next to him.

"You going to start your new life as a hairdresser?" I teased him, as he draped an arm around my waist, pulling me in closer.

"Hmm, I'll have to think about that," he murmured as he leaned in to plant a kiss on my lips. And, just like that, everything we had been talking about just vanished from my brain at once. Because we were here again, here together, and nothing else seemed to come close to mattering right now.

He pulled me down on to the bed beside him, wrapping his arms around me as though he never intended to let me go, and I sighed into the kiss, relief flooding through me. As long as we were together, I knew I could handle anything the world threw at us. We had each other, we would survive anything. I loved him. I knew I loved him. And I knew that he felt the same way about me, even if we hadn't said as much to each other yet. Sometimes, you didn't need to say a damn thing, you just needed to know, in your heart of hearts, that it was true, that you could share it in a kiss without worrying for a second about anything else.

He pulled back for a moment, looking deep into my eyes, and smiled.

"You have no idea how good it feels to have you back here," he murmured.

"Show me," I murmured right back, and he grinned as he leaned in to kiss me again – harder than before, his tongue slipping past my lips as he pressed his body to mine. I could already feel his cock stirring, and I hooked one leg over the top of his so I could grind against him passionately. He couldn't even imagine how much I had missed him in the time I had been away from him. But I intended to prove it to him, once and for all, make it so that he had no reason to doubt.

He pushed the robe away from my body, his mouth tracing down my skin and over my neck, lingering for a moment at my throat as though he was trying to steal my breath right out of my body. I groaned, cupping his head in my hands, the warmth of his lips on my skin enough to make everything else just vanish from my mind. This was the special power he had, to be able to make me drunk on my want for him to the point where nothing else mattered.

He continued down, rolling me on to my back as he pulled the robe off me, his lips tracing a line down my stomach, towards my mound. I couldn't take my eyes off of him – he flicked his up to meet mine, and I could see that flash of want in his face, a reminder of his need for me, how badly the two of us craved each other.

Finally, he landed between my thighs, parting my legs so that he could admire my pussy close-up – normally, I would have felt a little nervous at being so exposed, but with him, it was anything but. I knew I could trust him, totally and utterly, and that relief of giving myself, my pleasure over to him – it was everything.

He pressed his mouth to my pussy and I let out a long sigh of pleasure, my breath catching in the back of my throat as the delight of it coursed through my system. He always knew just what to do to me. His hands slid under my ass as he pulled me onto him properly, and I glanced down to steal a look at him between my legs like that. Damn, he looked perfect.

But he felt even better. His tongue swirled around my clit a few times before he drew it between his lips, applying the gentlest amount of pressure as he teased me. I groaned and arched my back from the bed so that I could press myself against him properly. How did he make it feel so good? He was so tender, kissing me down there as though he knew I could only take the slightest pressure, my body so over-sensitized just from his presence that it felt like my whole system was on fire.

I reached down to grip his hair, holding him in place as he started to apply more pressure with his tongue, and my mouth dropped open as I felt it increase, starting to grow and build between my thighs. The pleasure was delicious, but I needed more – enough that I would be able to forget entirely about the mess that surrounded us.

It consumed me. His hands dug into my ass as he pulled me on to him, as though he couldn't get enough of the taste of me. I knew how he felt. After so long apart, it felt as though I would never be able to get enough of him. I wanted to gorge myself on every part of him, the way he was feasting on my pussy right now...

The orgasm started to build inside of me, the pleasure and the pressure of everything I had attempted to hold back making it hard to think straight. Nothing mattered but the way that he made me feel, nothing could. His tongue swirled around my clit in long, slow strokes, and he let out a moan into my pussy, sending a coursing rush of pleasure through me all at once.

"Fuck," I groaned, one hand gripping the sheets as the other clutched to his hair. I needed this. I could feel my body tensing, clenching around him, my thighs pinning him in place as I got closer and closer to the edge. I was panting for air, gasping for breath, and soon, it hit me.

The orgasm rose up and over me like a wave, swallowing me whole so that I couldn't think about anything other than the pleasure as it rolled through me. He pulled back, my pussy pulsing where his tongue had just tasted me, and I groaned helplessly, my body convulsing with pleasure. I reached down for him, pulling him on top of me so I could taste my wetness on his lips, a reminder of where he had just been and what he had just done.

"Fuck me," I panted to him. I couldn't think of anything more important than that right now, and he didn't need telling twice; he pulled his cock from inside his pants and pressed himself to the entrance of my still-convulsing pussy, thrusting into me so hard that it made me cry out.

He wrapped himself around me as I wound my legs around his once more, pulling him deeper and deeper into me. He felt so perfect, it was almost more than I could take. The way we fit together, as though we had been made for each other – how did I think for a second that I could have married someone else? I was his. I belonged to him completely, the way my body craved his, the way I felt when we were together.

I held him close, inhaling the scent of his skin greedily as he fucked me. He felt so good I couldn't think straight, my body desperate for another orgasm, hungry for that new wave of pleasure. I squeezed my thighs around him, pulling him in deeper – I felt like I couldn't get enough of him, not even if I tried, the sheer intensity of it getting the better of me.

I had no idea how long we were tangled on that bed together, the two of us fucking like our lives depended on it. Because maybe they did – maybe there was some part of us that needed this assurance that we were together again, that we weren't always meant to come back to this point to find one another. But all that mattered was that he felt downright perfect inside of me, and I was here, with him, in his arms, close to him in the way I could only ever really be with the man I loved.

His breathing started to come harder and faster than before, and I knew that he was getting close. I wanted to feel him finish inside of me, letting him flood me with his seed to claim me as his own. My body cried out for that primal connection, something that I would never have given to anyone else. He pulled back, gazed into my eyes for a moment as he continued to move inside of me, and I bit my lip and then pulled him in for another kiss.

Our tongues danced together as he pushed himself deeper and deeper into me. I could feel his body tensing, my own responding in kind, as we both arched towards the release that we needed. I wanted to feel him inside of me, every part of him that I could, the passion and power of our coming together enough to wipe everything else off the face of the Earth. As far as I was concerned, it was just the two of us in the entire world right now, and that was exactly how I wanted it.

When he finished, I felt the warmth of him inside of me, and then my own body responded in kind. I moaned against his mouth as he stilled, letting my pussy contract in orgasm around his cock, as the two of us slowly, slowly came back down to Earth.

He planted one last kiss against my lips before he pulled back, allowing me to savor him for an instant before this was over, and then he flopped down into the bed next to me, cupping my face in his hands as he did so. I smiled, utterly sated, my body spent in the best way possible. I turned to him, found his eyes soft on mine as he looked at me.

"I love you," he murmured. And the words, though they were simple, meant everything in the world to me. I smiled and reached over to stroke his leg.

"I love you, too," I replied. He pulled me into his arms so that I could rest my head against his chest, and I closed my eyes and snuggled in close. I never wanted to be away from this man again, not as long as I lived. He was everything to me, and the closeness I felt when we were together was all that I needed to keep me sane.

These last few weeks might have been hell without him – but now that I was back where I belonged, in his arms, I knew nothing could take it away from me.

Chapter Twenty

Andreas

WHEN I WOKE THE NEXT morning, it was to the weight of the woman next to me in bed. And, as I opened my eyes to look over at her, I couldn't help but smile.

She was here. Next to me. My plan had worked, somehow. I knew Nikita or one of his men must have worked out that she had made a break for it, and I had no doubt that the city had exploded into chaos since she left. But here, now, it was hard to even think of that, because she was here with me, where she belonged, and the peace I felt looking at the soft rise and fall of her chest wiped everything else out of existence.

I reached over to stroke her face, but she didn't stir much. She must have been exhausted from everything that had happened. I hoped she would sleep all day, if that was what she needed – anything to allow her body to heal after everything she had been through.

We had told each other that we loved one another the night before, and I was so glad that it was out there at last. I did love her, more than I had loved anyone before in my life, and it would have felt wrong to keep that from her a second longer. I felt like we were meant to be together, something that I had never felt with anyone before, that solid, settled sureness I felt when I woke up next to her.

I leaned over to kiss her cheek, and her eyes fluttered open. She smiled at me, sleepy, and stretched out in the bed beside me.

"How did you sleep?" I asked her.

"Pretty well," she replied, her voice throaty from her slumber. She looked so fucking hot beside me that it was hard not to get distracted, but my phone buzzed on the bedside table and I went to check it at once.

It was a picture, courtesy of the driver Leo had sent to the city to pick up Dmitri. The sun was rising over the Manhattan bridge, and Dmitri was in the back of a car heading towards the edge of New York.

I showed the picture to Nadia.

"Look, your dad's getting out of town."

She looked over at the picture and frowned.

"I thought he was already gone?"

"He will be by this afternoon, that's all that matters," I promised her. "He's going to be out of the country by tonight, and there's no way for Nikita or anyone else to find out where he's staying."

She chewed her lip. She didn't look convinced. I couldn't say that I blamed her. After everything that had happened, it only seemed logical that she would have some doubts about the sureness of this plan. I just prayed she would trust me enough to see this through.

I pulled her against my chest, wrapping my arms around her. Kissing the top of her head, I did my very best to comfort her.

"Hey, you know you have nothing to worry about, right?" I asked her, and she managed to nod.

"Yeah, I think I'm starting to get that."

"Good."

She snuggled against me, draping her arm over my chest as though she never wanted to let me go. I knew how she felt – whatever it was, the connection between us now felt stronger than it had ever been, as though she had finally started to understand that I really meant it when I said that I would look out for her.

We rose from the bed after a few minutes, both of us too anxious to see what came next to spend more time hanging out and doing nothing. Today was the day that it all started, one way or another, that it all came to light, and I was determined to make sure that everything ran the way it was supposed to.

I made us a pot of coffee as I checked my phone to see if Leo had gotten in touch with me – I had no clue what he was planning to do in New York today, but I hoped he and his men were strong enough to handle whatever happened when Nikita found out that Nadia had been snatched right from under his nose.

"Do you think he's found out by now?" Nadia asked, shifting uncomfortably in her seat. I nodded.

"I think so," I murmured, coming over to join her. "But honestly – there's nothing he can do about it. He's just going to be pissed he can't see his plan through. You're safe. You and your father. Okay?"

"Okay," she breathed. I still hadn't told her the ins and outs of the plan that her captor had in place for her, because I figured she didn't need to hear something like that right now. I was sure she had guessed what he was willing to do to her. She didn't need me to drag it out again.

I brushed her hair back from her face, and she looked up at me and managed a small smile.

"Thank you for getting me out of there."

"If you thought I was going to let you marry that piece of shit," I told her, shaking my head, "you've got another thing coming."

She giggled.

"I didn't even think you would find out about it," she confessed. "I – I thought you would be done with me, after I left New York."

"I'm never going to be done with you, Nadia," I replied.

"You have no idea how glad I am to hear that," she murmured, and she smiled up at me. Fuck, when she smiled at me, it was like everything in the world just dropped away – everything fell back so I could be in this moment with her, so I could give myself over to the heaven of being in her company.

I made myself a coffee, and sat down with her at the table – I wanted to get her something to eat, but I was sure that she would have turned it down for the time being.

"So, what happens now?" she asked. I had tried to fill her in last night on as much as I could, about Leo and the FBI and the agents who had been working with us, but she seemed to have a hard time taking it all in.

"I think Leo is going to keep an eye on the wedding, or at least, what was meant to be the wedding," I explained. She nodded.

"And what happens then?"

"They're going to do their best to destabilize his position and make sure he doesn't turn it into an opportunity to cause more harm," I continued. "And after that..."

I trailed off. Honestly, what came after that scared me a little. I knew I had to be ready to fight, no matter what, but I had to believe Nikita would bring down hell on my head the first chance he got. He was a man who hated me with a real passion, and he was going to do everything that he could to make sure I didn't win this war between us.

"After that?" she pressed me, sounding concerned. She had good reason to be, heaven knew she did. I didn't want to have to involve her in any of this, but at the same time, leaving her out of the loop was going to make her feel like I didn't trust her.

"After that, we have to be ready to take him on ourselves," I replied. "The FBI are pulling their agents out of the field to leave a clear path. And then we can do what needs to be done."

A shadow flickered across her face, and I could see the fear in her eyes. She knew what that meant, even if she wished she didn't. Even if I wished that I could protect her from this, keep her from falling deeper into this mess that she had been dragged into, I needed her to know what we were up against.

"And that means war, right?" she asked. I nodded.

"That means war."

It was the first time I had said it out loud, and it sent a shiver down my spine to hear it. I had to be ready to fight this man, take him on in any way that he tried to throw at me. I wasn't scared, not for myself – I could handle me – but for the people he might come after as a way of trying to harm me. Men like that, they were always willing to do whatever it took to win, and I had no doubt that he would come gunning for Nadia and her father to make a point about what I did and didn't have over him.

"But you're going to be okay," I promised her. "I'm going to keep you safe. You and your father. You're here with me, he's way out in Vancouver, or he will be soon. You have nothing to worry about, okay?"

"Okay," she replied, letting out a breath I didn't even realize she had been holding. I wanted to pull her into my arms again, but that might have given her reason to think she should have been scared. I needed to play it cool right now, make it obvious that nothing that was happening was going to impact her.

A small smile flickered across her lips, and she glanced up at me.

"I wish I could see the look on his face when he realizes that I'm gone," she remarked, mischief playing in her eyes. I laughed.

"Yeah, wish I could see that too," I agreed. "He's going to be furious."

"But he knows there's nothing he can do," she continued, the smile spreading further. I was glad she seemed to be taking some level of glee in what was going on, she deserved to – we both did, after what we had been through. I didn't know the details of everything Nikita had done to her, but I doubted it was anything good. The mere thought of him laying a hand on her sparked my anger to a point where I could hardly control it, and I was sure nothing good would come from making her recount the details if she didn't offer them up herself.

My phone buzzed, pulling me out of the conversation for a moment, and I snatched it up to answer it at once. It was likely Leo, with some information about what was happening in the city. I could practically picture the chaos now, the shit that Nikita was spreading over New York as he tried to get back the bride who had abandoned him. He really thought he could just take what he wanted from her, but she had pushed back and made sure that he lost out at the last minute.

"Hello?"

"Hello."

The voice on the other end of the line sent a sharp shiver down my spine, and Nadia must have been able to see it – she mouthed *who is it* at me, but I held my hand up, telling her silently that I would be with her as soon as I could.

Because if this was who I thought it was – we had some serious issues here. Some serious fucking issues.

"Who is this?" I demanded. I needed to know for sure before I jumped to any conclusions, but I was already pretty certain I knew.

"You know."

"Who is—"

"This is Nikita," he growled down the line, voice brimming with a rage I had never heard before in my life. "And if you don't put her on the line in the next ten seconds, I'm going to find you, and I'm going to speak to her myself. You understand me?"

Chapter Twenty-One

Nadia

AS SOON AS I HEARD the voice at the other end of the line, I knew the call was for me.

Andreas tried to slide his eyes from mine, so that he didn't have to look at the shock and horror on my face, but there was no hiding it. It was obvious. My mouth dropped open – how had he been able to find us?

I could hear him saying my name, over and over again, the shape of me in his mouth enough to make my stomach turn. I wanted this to be over. I wanted it done, now. If he had to speak to me, then I would do it myself, make sure that he had no reason to come down here and shatter the small piece of serenity Andreas and I had been able to create together.

I rose to my feet and held my hand out for the phone.

"Let me speak to him," I told Andreas, attempting as best I could to keep the shake out of my voice. He shook his head and covered the speaker.

"I can handle this—"

"He wants to talk to me, doesn't he?" I demanded, and Andreas hesitated for a moment before nodding.

"Yes, but—"

"Then let me speak to him."

He eyed me for a moment, and I could tell that he didn't want to hand over that phone right now. But I wasn't going to give him a choice. I needed to speak to him, I needed to make sure he understood

135

how serious I was about leaving him behind. Nikita needed to hear it from me directly, and I would ensure he had no doubts about why I had made a run for it.

Andreas handed me the phone, and I lifted it to my ear.

"Nikita?"

My voice was shaking, and I hated myself for giving him even a hint of fear. I wanted to be strong in the face of this man, strong enough to prove to him that he couldn't do anything to scare me.

"Nadia," he replied. His tone was unreadable, but I had a good idea of what he was feeling right now. He'd had everything just the way he'd wanted it, and then I had run for the hills and left him with nothing. He was furious, and he, frankly, had every right to be. But I wasn't going to let that change my position, or what I had done. When I got out of there, I had done it for me, done it to make sure I didn't get trapped in his nightmarish fantasy of what he had planned for us. Andreas had hinted at what Nikita was going to do, the plans he had as soon as that ring was on my finger, and it was clear that I wouldn't even have had time to take him out myself before he'd done the same to me.

"I wish you were here with me now, my darling," he told me. His voice was laced with venom now, even though his words seemed sweet on the surface.

"I think I'm better off here," I replied, curtly. I wasn't going to let him sweet-talk me. He had never had me, and I wasn't about to let him think he had.

"We could have had everything, you know," he told me, and I could have mistaken the edge to his voice for genuine sadness – if I hadn't known what he had been planning to do to me as soon as he got the chance.

"We could have had a real life together," he continued, almost wistful now, and I bit back a laugh at the mere thought of it. A life? After he had forced me into a marriage with him? What sort of life did he think that would be for me? A life that I wanted? The mere thought of his hands on me had been enough to send me running, and he thought I would have stuck around for a *life?*

"You mean, after you took me out at our wedding reception?" I replied icily. I wasn't going to let him spin this. He wasn't some spurned lover, left behind by a heartless bride-to-be. He was a monster, a would-be rapist who would have taken from me anything that he could. He knew that as well as I did, but he didn't care to admit to any of it. He would have hurt me and not felt an ounce of remorse, because, where he came from, as long as there was a ring on that finger, anything went.

"You have no idea what you've gotten yourself into," he growled, his tone changing on a dime. This was the Nikita that hid underneath everything else, the one he tried his best to hide from everyone. He might have wanted to pretend that he had some small modicum of control over himself, but he didn't. He would lash out at me and everyone else around me to prove that I was wrong for leaving him behind.

"I'm happier here than I ever would have been with you," I fired back. Riling him up was the last thing I needed to do, but it felt good to spit back at him everything I had been so carefully keeping to myself all this time.

"You won't have it much longer," he warned me. "Your father—"

"My father is safe," I told him, proudly. "You have no idea where he is. Did you have anyone keep an eye on him?"

I heard silence, and then mumbling, as he talked to someone off the call – and then, a grunt of anger as he realized that I was telling the truth.

"Just because you've gotten your father out of the city doesn't mean anything," he warned me. "I'll find him. I'll find both of you. And I'm not going to stop until your entire fucking family is wiped off the face of the Earth, do you hear me?"

The fury in his voice terrified me, but I bit back my fear. I wasn't going to give him the satisfaction of knowing he had scared me. I was stronger than he thought I was, stronger than anything he could throw at me, and I knew I could take whatever he tried to scare me with.

"Good fucking luck," I spat back, and before I could say another word, Andreas leaned over to take the phone from me again. I didn't blame him – I wasn't exactly doing a great job in trying to get anything useful out of him.

"What the hell do you want?" Andreas asked as he switched the phone on to speaker so we could both hear what he had to say.

"I want to end this," Nikita growled to him.

"We can," Andreas promised him. "We can end this tonight. Today. Just the two of us."

I stared at him. Did he know who he was dealing with here? Nikita was the kind of monster who would do everything he could to take what he wanted from the people around him, and if he wanted blood, he would make sure he got it. No way was I going to let Andreas walk out of that door and to some meeting with just Nikita. He would be killed.

"Just the two of us?" Nikita repeated after him, a mocking tone to his voice as though he found the mere thought of it amusing.

"Just us," Andreas replied. Nikita snorted with amusement, though there was no warmth to his voice.

"I want her there, too," he replied. "I want Nadia there, so she can see when I paint the floor with your blood."

My stomach turned. I couldn't be close to that man again. But at the same time, there was no way I was going to let Andreas walk in there alone. I needed to be with him, needed to make sure he got out in one piece – I was scared, but that didn't mean I was scared enough to let him face Nikita alone.

"She can be there," Andreas replied, and he reached out to squeeze my hand. I shook my head. We couldn't do this. Maybe he was just saying what he thought Nikita wanted to hear to get this over with, but there was no way in fucking hell I was going to let him meet with Nikita in person. No fucking way.

"Good," Nikita replied. "It's only fair that you get to be with the woman you love in your last moments, don't you think?"

I shivered. Nikita spoke with such sureness, as though he knew without a shadow of a doubt that he had us all right where he wanted us. I hated this. I thought I had left him behind when I had managed to escape the horror of that wedding, but it was clear that I was anything but free of him.

"Come to your old club," he continued. "The burned one. I'll meet you there in two hours. Bring her with you, or we have no deal. You understand?"

"I understand," Andreas replied. His voice sounded hollow. I prayed it was because he didn't have any intention of going through with this, but the more I sat there and listened, the more sure I was that he intended to do it.

He hung up the phone, and I clasped his face in my hands at once.

"Andreas, you can't do this," I pleaded with him. "Please, you have to listen to me—"

"Nadia," he murmured, and he planted a kiss on my lips to silence me. Even now, in the midst of all of this, I couldn't deny the sweet power of his kiss.

"We have to go," he told me, cupping my cheek in his palm. "I know you don't want to. And trust me, if there was any way I could go through with this without having you there, I would. But we have to get this over with."

"I thought you said there was going to be a war," I told him. "That doesn't mean you have to be the one fighting it, does it?"

"There was always going to be a war, but this way, we might be able to shut it down before anyone else gets hurt," he explained. "I owe that to my men. And to this city. If the Serbians start something, we might not have a chance to pull out, and the chaos they could cause..."

He trailed off, shook his head. I could see the doubt as it flickered over his face, the fear. I didn't want him to have to do this. I had spent more time with Nikita than him, and I knew what that psycho was capable of. I trusted Andreas, I loved him, but he wasn't able to predict the kind of violence that Nikita would mete out when he got the chance.

"It's what I have to do," he told me firmly, and I knew there was going to be no changing his mind. I could have spent this entire day arguing with him, but it wouldn't have meant anything. He wanted this over.

"As soon as this is done, we get to be together properly," he murmured. I shook my head.

"And what if I lose you?" I demanded, my voice cracking. "I can't lose you again, Andreas, not after everything that happened…"

He pulled me into his arms and kissed me again, the kind of kiss that seemed to knock the breath right out of my body, and all I could do was hang on to him for dear life and kiss him back. I had no idea what was going to come next, not really, but maybe it didn't matter.

Maybe, as long as I had him here in my arms, I could just focus on the relief of his closeness, and let go of anything else.

No matter how scared I was of what Nikita was going to do to us next.

Chapter Twenty-Two

Andreas

AS THE CAR PULLED TO a halt outside the remains of my old club, I shot a look at Nadia.

She was terrified. I could see it written all over her face, and I wondered if I had made the wrong choice bringing her here in the first place. I could have left her behind, told her to wait for me back at the safehouse, but I was sure she wouldn't have taken that for an answer.

Besides, Nikita wanted her here, and he wouldn't go through with whatever he had in mind unless I did. I was sure he was going to turn this on its head, try something to take me out, but I had to put what little trust I had in him on the line here.

I hated having to give him anything, to be honest. The thought of having to offer this guy a single shred of kindness was enough to make me feel ill. He had done nothing but hurt the people I cared about, and he wasn't going to stop until I put a close on this chapter for good.

"Are you sure you want to do this?" Nadia asked. She hadn't said much over the course of our journey together – there wasn't much to say – but I could tell that her mind was working at a million miles per hour as she tried to figure everything out.

"I don't want to," I admitted. "But I have to. It's the only way we can stop this war before it starts."

She nodded, chewed her lip.

"Okay."

"You sure?"

"Not really," she confessed. "But if that's what we have to do, I'll do it."

I climbed out of the car and opened the door for her. I had let Leo know what we were doing, and I was sure he was watching somewhere. I didn't bother looking around for him, knowing that it would have given away my new allyship, but I was certain I could feel eyes on us right now.

We headed inside the club, Nadia hanging onto my arm as tight as she could. I didn't want her to let go. I knew we were about to face down some serious danger, and I needed her to understand that I was going to do everything I was able to in order to keep her safe. I hated that she had to be here at all, but I would rather that she was with me. I wouldn't have trusted Nikita not to try and steal her away the moment I turned my back on her, used this encounter as a distraction to go through with the wedding that she had humiliated him by not turning up for.

When we arrived inside what was left of the main hall, I couldn't help but remember the first time Nadia and I had met. When she had danced with me, pressed her body to mine, the way she had looked into my eyes as though she wanted me, even then. All those months ago, I hadn't been sure if she meant it or not, but now, I could see that it had been real – that we had been real. From day one. We had been real, and everything we'd shared since then had been building on that intense chemistry that we had felt from the first moment we had met one another.

Nikita, it seemed, hadn't lived up to the agreement that we had made; a half-dozen of his men were flanking him as we emerged into his vicinity. Most of them were armed, and all of them had their eyes trained on me. I felt Nadia stiffen next to me, and I squeezed her hand. I didn't want her to give away a single shred of fear in that moment. We had to be strong, both of us, present a united front. That was the only way we were going to get through this alive.

"I see you didn't honor the rules of our arrangement," I told Nikita, who was looking at me like he wanted to rip my head from my shoulders right where I stood. I didn't blame him. I had the woman he wanted more than anything on my arm, and he knew he would never get her to look at him the way she looked at me. It must have made him sick. I hoped it did.

"Didn't think you would be stupid enough to believe I'd stick by them," he sneered. He had this dark coldness to him now, something even more dangerous than before, as though he had nothing left to lose. His plans were already spinning out of his control, and he had no idea how to get them back on track. If I could keep pushing him, I might get him off it for good.

"You at least willing to meet with me alone?" I asked. "Your men can wait here. I brought Nadia. You said you wanted her to see this, right?"

I was trying to keep my cool, but I could feel the anger rising inside of me, the anger at the thought that he had tried to make her his. He had no idea the kind of woman she was, the strength that she possessed, and he didn't understand on any fucking level how hard I would fight to make sure that I didn't lose her.

"If you'd like to do this in private, we can," Nikita replied, and he nodded to one of his men, who pulled open a door next to us so we could step inside. It was my old office, the very same one Nadia and I had first kissed in. The memories were still fresh in my mind. If I didn't make it out of here, then I knew, at least, I would have that to go out with – the sweetness of her lips on mine, the way she had kissed me like she knew we were meant to be something together.

I followed him into the office, and Nadia clung to my arm and stuck right behind me. I wished I could have told her that she had nothing to worry about, but it didn't work like that. Neither of us knew how this was going to turn out. And yet, despite it all, there was a wash of calm in my chest. Whatever happened, I knew that I had won. I had

Nadia by my side. She had chosen me, and nothing Nikita could do or say was going to change that, no matter how much he wanted it to.

"What do you need from me?" Nikita asked, spreading his hands wide as I closed the door behind us. I knew his men were just outside. It didn't make much difference to shut them out like that, but there was no way that I was going to let them see what I was going to do. If he wanted a fight, then I was going to give him a fucking fight – but it was going to be between the two of us.

"I want you to prove that you can do anything without your men there to protect you," I replied, cocking an eyebrow. I dropped Nadia's hand, glanced over my shoulder to silently tell her to take a step back. I didn't want her to get hurt, and given how monstrous Nikita was, I had no doubt that he would lash out at her if he thought he could get what he wanted.

"You really think I can't handle myself?" Nikita growled, getting right up in my face.

"That's how you've been acting," I replied, as calmly as I could. I didn't feel scared. I had something he would never have – I had Nadia. Willingly. Loving me. I had won.

"If you really believe I can't wipe some little fucker like you off the map, you're more delusional than I thought—" he started, but before he could get any further, I shoved him. Hard.

He stumbled back a few paces, looking furious. I almost had to laugh – he looked so ridiculous like that, affronted at me daring to lay a hand on him even though he knew as well as I did that this was what we were here for. Nadia drew back against the door. She had never liked the violence, and I didn't blame her. I wished I could have spared her this. But Nikita needed to understand that this was what she had chosen - even if he won, she had still picked me, and nothing he could do would change that.

And with that, the fight began. He swung a fist at me - I managed to duck mostly out of the way, but it caught the side of my jaw and sent me spinning. Even though he was older than me, he was still strong, and it was clear that he wasn't going to let this go.

But I had the fury of knowing everything that he had done to Nadia behind me, and I wasn't about to let that drop. I spun around and shoved him again, this time aiming a knee into his stomach to send him crashing over to the floor. His head slammed back against the concrete wall, and he let out a groan that turned into a rising wail of anger as he climbed back to his feet and dove at me again.

I dodged him this time, catching myself on the edge of the desk as I nearly went careering on to the floor, but managing to stay upright. Nadia was pressed against the wall, trying to stay as far out of it as she could, and I didn't blame her. She looked terrified. I was doing this for her – I was ending this for her, because she deserved to be able to go on with her life without having to fight for every breath she and her father took.

Nikita was strong, and he didn't back down easily, even as blood clotted at the back of his shaven head where he had crashed against the wall. He flung himself at me, over and over, like he was trying to wipe me off the face of the Earth once and for all.

But his desperation got the better of him, and soon, I found myself with the upper hand, thrusting him down to the floor one last time and standing over him. His eyes were glazed, his face bloody, his lip swollen where I had landed a particularly bad hit. He was still burning with anger, but he knew, as he looked up at me, that I had won.

I turned back to Nadia. This was up to her now. If she wanted me to end him, then I would do it, I would do it in an instant, but I needed to know that she wanted it as much as I did. I wasn't going to do this if it meant scaring her off for good.

She nodded. I could still see how scared she was, but she knew this was what we had to do. We had to end him, right here and now, if we had any hope of making it out of this mess in one piece.

I grabbed the desk, heaved it on to its edge so that it was dangling a mere inch or two from his face – his eyes were blurry now, his body starting to shut down, but he still closed his eyes before I brought it crashing down on his head.

The sound made my stomach turn, the sickness boiling in my veins. But, when I looked down at him, his skull crushed beneath the desk, I knew it was over. He was gone. Dead.

I turned back to Nadia and pulled her into my arms. She was trembling so hard she was nearly vibrating, but I kept her close, not letting her go. I had no idea what was going to happen now, if we were going to make it out of here, if his men were going to gun us down right then and there the moment they realized I had taken out their beloved leader – but as long as I had her, I knew I had made the right choice.

"Is he gone?" she asked, her voice so tiny it sounded like it had come from some place buried deep inside of her. I nodded.

"He's gone," I promised her, smoothing her hair. "He's gone."

"How do we get out of here?" she asked me, and I shook my head.

"I don't know," I confessed. I had thought Nikita would stick by his promise and come without back-up, but they were waiting just outside the door, and I had no doubt that they would be willing to do whatever needed to be done when they realized what had happened.

She leaned her head against mine and closed her eyes. I knew that she was coming to terms with it, with what I had just told her. That we might not get out of here in one piece. We had no idea how this was going to go. But he was gone. We were together, and he was gone, and for now, that was all that seemed to matter in the world.

She planted her lips to mine, and her kiss told me everything I needed to know. Whatever had happened to lead us to this point, it had been right, because we were together. When she pulled back, she gazed into my eyes and nodded.

"We have to get out," she told me. "Or try, at least."

"And if we don't?" I asked her. I needed her to know that it was a possibility, at least, no matter how much I wished I could have promised her something different. She grimaced.

"My father's safe, isn't he?"

"Totally."

"Then we can do whatever we want," she replied. She planted a hand on the door and took a deep breath. And then, she pushed it open.

I waited for the gunfire to start – waited for something to happen, at least, as we dove out from the office. The men out there, as soon as they saw that Nikita wasn't with us, it would be game fucking over, they would shut us down right then and there.

But instead, they had turned outwards. Something else had caught their attention. One of them lifted a gun and fired towards the top of the building, and the others followed suit. I didn't need telling twice.

I grabbed her hand and sprinted towards the door.

I wasn't going to wait for another chance to get out of there. We needed to run. We needed to get as far from here as possible, as fast as we could. I had no idea what was going on, but I wasn't much willing to sit around and wait for it to unfold.

"What's happening?" Nadia demanded, but I shook my head. I didn't have time to explain anything to her, not that there was much I could have made sense of anyway.

"It doesn't matter," I replied as I tugged her towards the door. "We just have to get the fuck out of here."

Chapter Twenty-Three

Nadia

AS WE SPRINTED OUT of the remains of that club, I clung to his hand for dear life and prayed that we would make it out in one piece.

I had no idea what was happening, or why – I just knew that we needed to get as far from here as possible, and keep running even then. Who were the men firing at Nikita's bodyguards? I had no idea, and I figured I wasn't meant to know. All that mattered was that Nikita was dead, and that we weren't being shot full of bullets as we tried to make our escape.

Outside the door, on the street, I looked this way and that, terrified that someone might be waiting to take us down. But, instead of more of Nikita's men, the street was packed with police cars, armed men in uniform pouring out of their vehicles to rush into the building. What was going on? How had this happened? My mind was spinning as I tried to make sense of it, but I knew there was nothing I could do to assign a meaning to all of this.

"Come on, we don't have time to stop," Andreas told me urgently, and he pulled me towards the car we had arrived in

"Where are we going?" I asked, and he shook his head.

"I don't know," he admitted. "But far from here. Far, far from here."

"Who are those people in there?" I asked, nodding back towards the building. "Are those the FBI guys you were working with?"

"I have no idea," he replied, as he pulled open the door, and hustled me inside. "Come on. I'm not waiting to find out how many of them are on our side."

He pulled out of the parking lot of what had once been the club I had worked at, and we hit the road. I rolled down the window, let the wind whoosh through my hair; I couldn't believe what had just happened. Nikita, he was gone, he was really gone. All that time I had spent sure that I didn't have a hope in hell of getting away from him, and it was over. He was out of my life now, and nothing was going to pull him back in. I was safe. Finally, really, truly, utterly, safe.

It was like a weight had lifted from my shoulders that I had never known was there till now. I didn't think I would be able to handle the horror of watching someone killed in front of me, but when it was the man who had intended to use me the way that Nikita had, I didn't care. No, more than that – I was glad he was gone. The world was better off without him, I was sure of it, and the sooner that it even forgot he had been a part of it, the better.

Andreas reached over to put a hand on my leg, his eyes still on the road ahead of him. I didn't even know where we were going, and I doubted that he did, either. He just knew that we had to drive, had to keep driving to get the fuck out of here. The sooner this city was behind us, the better. The sooner we would be able to forget that any of this had happened in the first place.

"Are you okay?" he asked softly, and I nodded.

"Yeah, I am," I replied, surprised at how honest I could be with him. I didn't have to hide it – didn't have to pretend anything any longer. I had been putting on a front for such a long time that I had almost forgotten what it felt like to just be straight with myself, with the people around me.

"It's okay if you're not—"

"I know," I assured him. "But I am. I really am."

I smiled at him, and he smiled back – and then, his phone rang in his pocket. He took it out, put it on speaker, and planted it on the dashboard in front of him.

"Hello?"

"Andreas," a man's voice came down the line. "This is Leo. Where are you?"

"We're getting out of the city," he replied.

"Good," the man replied. "You should get as far from here as you can. We have some safehouses out on Florida right now, you can wait there till we have a chance to re-calibrate and—"

"I don't want to deal with this shit anymore," Andreas replied, cutting him off mid-flow. "I'm not going to Florida, Leo. And I'm not going to sit around and wait for you to give me the go-ahead. We're getting out of the city, we're getting out of all of this."

"And what about the Salieri family?" Leo demanded. I stared at Andreas, trying to work out if he really meant any of this. Surely, he couldn't just leave it all behind, could he?

"We're done," he replied, his eyes narrowing as they pinned on to the road in front of him. "We're out. We're taking the money, and we're starting over. You won't hear from us again."

"Andreas, I—" Leo started, but Andreas turned off the phone before he could say anything else. I could sense the exhilaration pumping through his veins at that moment, and I wondered if he really meant it.

"Are we – are we really doing this?" I asked him, barely even daring to hope that it was real. He nodded. He reached for my hand and held on to it tightly, as though making sure I was really there with him and I wasn't going to go anywhere. As though I could have, in the face of everything that was happening – as though I would have. I needed him. I needed him here with me and I knew that he needed me just as much, and that nothing was going to change that.

"Yeah, we are," he replied, and there was a sureness to his voice that told me everything I needed to know. We were together now. We were really, honestly, truly doing this, and I wanted to, more than anything in the world. I wanted to feel his touch, feel the sweetness of him close to me, and know that I could hold on to him with everything that I had. No matter how hard it might be, no matter how crazy the circumstances that had brought us to this moment, we were together now, and I would hold onto that with everything I had.

"Where are we going to go?" I asked him, and he paused, considering.

"Well, we need to get our passports and everything first," he replied. "And then, we need to go to your father. Get him out of Vancouver."

"After that?" I asked. He pulled my hand to his lips, planted a kiss against my knuckles.

"We can go anywhere you want," he told me. And suddenly, the world seemed to open up in front of me in a way it never had before in my life – and everything, everything I had been trying for so long to run from was here in front of me. I could finally move forward without having to hide myself away. I had survived the worst that life could throw at me, and now, with the man I loved, I could take on anything that came next.

"I've got a few ideas," I murmured, and I bit my lip as I ran through the possibilities. A whole world in front of me, the freedom to do anything that I wanted to try.

And the person I loved most in the world next to me to make it happen.

Six weeks later

The warmth of the Gold Coast sun blazed down on us, as I took a sip of the cocktail that I had been working on for the last half-hour or so. Did it get any better than this?

I stretched out on the enormous beach chair that was propped up next to the pool and sighed. I could get used to this. Which I was going to have to, if we were really going to make this place our home. I had every intention of staying here, at least for a little while; even after the first month had passed, I was still finding so much more to explore in Brisbane, and I didn't want to move on until I'd seen every corner that I could.

Beside me, Andreas lazily reached over to take my hand, and I flashed him a smile.

"You all good?" he asked me, and I nodded.

"Yeah, I really am," I replied, and I meant it.

Hard to believe that, merely a few weeks ago, we had been trapped in the chaos that New York city had dropped on our heads. It was crazy to imagine it had been so recent. It felt like it came from a whole other life now, as though it had happened to someone else entirely. Another girl, another life, another time. That was all behind me now.

We had made the run to Australia as soon as we picked up my father from Vancouver; we needed to leave that part of the world for a while, and this seemed like the best way that we could do that. As far removed from everything that we had known as possible, with as much space between our old lives and our new ones as we could get. My father had had a hard time letting go of the store back in New York, but I reminded him that my mother had always wanted to travel – she would have told him, in no uncertain terms, to fly all the way across the world if he had the chance, and he knew it.

"She would have wanted us to go on a real adventure," he had told me, as we had been sitting in the lounge waiting for our plane to leave. I grinned at him.

"I know she would," I agreed, and I leaned over to give him a hug. I was so relieved that he was here with me. I had thought that I might lose him, but now, with him right next to me, I knew I never would. He was safe, we both were.

And so was Andreas. He had taken all of his family's fortune and moved it to a bank account out here, and had basically shut down what remained of the Salieri family's legacy in New York. I was sure it would be hard for him, but he had told me that he had an easier time with all of it than he thought he would.

"I just... I think I've been holding onto what I thought my father would want from me all this time," he explained to me. "And now, I can finally let it go. I don't need to hang onto it anymore. He would have wanted me to live a real life, outside of all this mess, and now I've met you... I can."

My heart was so full when he talked to me like that. Now that we didn't have the pressure of Nikita or anyone else behind us, he was free to be the sweet romantic that he always had been. And damn, was he good at the romance side of this; he had picked out the most beautiful villa for us, one that overlooked the stunning beaches and the shimmering blue water of the sea that lapped up against the coast, and had decorated it with pictures of me and my family, which he had managed to get from my father. It already felt like home to me, especially given our access to the beautiful pool on the roof terrace.

That was my favorite place to be in the world right now. I loved just people-watching, and feeling like I could truly fade into the background here. I was the same as anyone else. Nobody looked twice at me, nobody had any reason to, and that was just the way I wanted to keep it.

We had taken on new names, at least when we were out and about – I was Elise, and Andreas went by Andrew. To anyone who might have seen us together, eating ice cream on the beach just like we had done back in Miami, we were the same as any other young couple here. Just a pair of people, making their way through this city, finding a home somewhere new. They would never have to know about the reality of everything we had left behind, and that was just how I liked it. Let it be our history – let it stay beyond the walls of this place, so we could truly start over.

And now, we were going to make this real. The day had come – we were getting married. I was officially going to be his wife, and I couldn't believe that it was really happening.

We had promised each other something simple, something quick, something that would tie us together without all the pomp and ceremony that normally came with a wedding this wealthy. I had thought

I would be more nervous at the notion of spending the rest of my life with him, committing to him in this way, but if anything, it just felt... right. Like I belonged there with him. The two of us, for everything that we had been through, had always been coming to this point, always been finding a way back to this spot so we could spend our lives together. I just hadn't realized it for a long time.

But I was going to put that right today. Andreas was chatting with the priest over by the edge of the balcony, and my father was sipping on a drink as he looked out over the sea beyond us – something non-alcoholic, since he had quit drinking for good, for the sake of his health. And damn, it made me happy to know he was taking that stuff seriously. That he really believed he had a reason to look after himself, after everything that had happened. He was already starting to look better, the sunshine giving him a warm tan, but more than anything, it was the weight of it all lifting from his shoulders that seemed to be making the biggest difference.

He was beyond excited that I was getting married, even though I kept telling him that we weren't going to be doing anything too extreme; he had made it pretty clear he would do most anything he could to ensure that it went well, and I had tried to convince him that he didn't need to get so over-invested in it. This was just a chance for Andreas and I to announce our commitment to each other to the world, we weren't making much more of it than that.

"But you'll be married, my little girl, getting married," he told me, shaking his head, misty-eyed. "I wish your mother was here to see this..."

"I think she is, somewhere," I replied. I meant it – more than ever now, I felt like my mom was watching over me. I knew she would have liked Andreas, and the two of them would have had a good time together. I hoped she approved of my choice of husband. She might have had doubts about what he did for a living, but that was behind him now. He would turn his attention to something new eventually, but the life that had caused us so much trouble in the first place, I was sure he was done with it for good.

And if he wasn't... well, at least I would be there to keep him on the right path. I knew I could help him make something of his family name. And since I was soon going to call it my own, I had even more investment in making sure that it remained as strong as it ever had been.

"Are you ready?" Andreas asked me, lifting a hand to shield himself from the sun as he peered down at me. I was just wearing a bikini and a robe, nothing fancy – I had thought about going out to get a dress, but then I'd been reminded of everything that had happened with Nikita and had thought better of it. For that wedding, the man I had meant to be married to had wanted me to doll myself up into someone I wasn't. Here, now, I knew that Andreas only wanted me as I was.

"Yeah, I am," I replied, smiling up at him. He offered me a hand to help me up, and I took it. His hand in marriage, I supposed. Damn, I couldn't believe this was really happening, but I knew I didn't want anything else in the world right now. We were meant for this, meant for each other, meant to connect on this level, and I wasn't going to let anything get in the way of it.

The priest was waiting over by the pool, at the edge of the balcony, and the sun was beaming down on the sea beyond us; it looked almost like something from a fantasy, as though it couldn't possibly be real. Or maybe that was just how I felt right now.

We held hands as we exchanged our vows, and I looked him in the eyes and wondered how I had managed to find a man like this. A man who was willing to go as far as he had to keep me safe, to protect me, to love me – and my family. I was never going to let him go. These vows captured some small part of what I felt, at least, some part of our connection, but it went deeper than that. We were meant to be, had been from the moment we met, and now that I could see it, I wasn't going to let it go.

"I do," he murmured back to me, and he leaned in to plant a kiss on my lips. I closed my eyes and wrapped my arms around him, smiling into our embrace, unable to hold it back – unable to keep myself from falling in love with him all over again. He was it – the man of my dreams, the man who I was going to spend the rest of my life with.

And, as he pulled back and gazed into my eyes, I knew he felt it too. All the passion, all the love, all the connection. All the want and desire and need. And most of all – the certainty. The certainty that we had made the right choice. Because we had ended up here, and this was, more than anything, where we belonged.

Chapter Twenty-Four

Andreas

"COME ON," I MURMURED to her, as I hustled her up the stairs to our bedroom.

"That's no way to speak to your wife," she giggled as she hitched up the robe she was wearing in order to take the stairs better.

"I'll speak to my wife however I like," I joked, and I caught her at the top of the stairs and pulled her into my arms for a kiss.

She smiled against my lips, and I held her close, not wanting to let her go. I couldn't believe it – we were really married. She was my wife. And now that I had her all to myself, after an evening of drinking and talking and laughing with her father, I was going to show her just how much that meant to me.

I scooped her up into my arms and she laughed as she hung on to me for dear life, holding me close as she buried her face into my neck. She was just wearing a bikini and a light robe that showed off every inch of her gorgeous body, and it had taken everything in me not to drag her up here for us to enjoy our wedding night way sooner than I had.

The doors to the balcony in our bedroom were thrown open, and I carried her outside so that we could look down on to the sea below us.

"It's so beautiful," she murmured to me, leaning her head back against my chest once I put her back on her feet. I wound my arms around her waist and kissed her neck.

"Not nearly as beautiful as you."

"Hey, have you always been this cheesy, or did I just notice it now?" She giggled as I brushed my lips along her jaw and finally found her mouth again.

That seemed enough to keep her quiet. I pushed the robe away from her body so I could touch her properly. Her skin felt perfect beneath my fingertips, something made just for me. I wanted to feast on her, gorge myself until I couldn't take any more, and I knew she felt the same way. These last few weeks together, they had just confirmed everything that I had already known, that our connection ran deeper than anything that I had ever felt with anyone before, and that nothing would come close to matching what we had.

She moaned softly against my lips as I pushed down her bikini bottoms, grinding against her perfect ass. I was just wearing trunks, but they felt like far too much in the way of the fabric right now. She reached behind herself to guide them down a little, and as soon as she felt my bare cock nestled against her, she smiled.

"You feel so good," she groaned, and I pulled her flush against me. It was like I couldn't get close enough to her, as though nothing would pull the two of us near enough to one another. I loved this feeling, this sensation of her bottom next to mine cock, and I knew that she could feel it, too – feel that rush of want, need, desire, that came mixed up with all the love we had for each other.

"Please, fuck me," she murmured.

"Here?" I asked. Even though we were high up over the city, someone could still look up and see us. She nodded.

"I want everyone here to know that I'm yours," she replied, her eyes pinned to mine as she spoke. I kissed her again, harder this time, the thrill of what she'd just said to me rushing through my body. My cock was swollen and hard and I took it into my hand, guided it against her pussy – she arched her back, gripped tight to the balcony in front of her, and let out a sigh of pleasure as I pushed into her.

She felt perfect. I would never get over how well our bodies fit together, as though they had been made for this. I watched as her eyes softened and closed while I moved in her, long, deep strokes as I fucked her right there in front of the entire city. So everyone would know she was mine, that she belonged to me.

This was my wife. My woman. She was mine now, all mine, and I belonged to her in just the same way. Our connection was sealed for good, and I would never let her go, knew that she would never let me slip through her fingers, either. I moved my hand up her body, fingers skimming her throat just barely, and she gasped, dipping her mouth to draw them inside.

The feel of her warm tongue against my fingertips lit me up, and I started going harder, harder. I was all the way inside of her, buried to the hilt, not holding back, and I could tell she didn't want me to. There was nothing to hide anymore, nothing to hold back from each other. It was all out there now, blatant, no secrets. Just the way I had always wanted it.

She sucked on my fingers as I slammed into her, harder, harder, filling her in long, deep strokes that had her legs trembling in a matter of minutes. Down below us, the world moved on unknowing, but up here, the two of us indulged in each other like it was our last night on Earth.

Or maybe our first night together, the way we were always meant to be. I wrapped an arm around her waist to pull her back on to me, so close that I couldn't hold back anymore, and I watched as her body spasmed around me, her system finally giving in to the pleasure we could share with each other.

I held myself deep inside of her as I came, filling her with my seed – I wanted that bonding, that deep passion to pull us together, and I could feel it forming as I held her close to me. I kissed her shoulder, tasting her skin, needing to gorge myself on as much of her as I could.

Slowly, slowly, I moved out of her, drawing my fingers out of her mouth as I did so, and she panted for breath as she clung on to the balcony for support.

"You okay?" I asked her, and she nodded, smiling at me.

"Just... need to lie down, I think," she replied, and I didn't need telling twice. I scooped her up into my arms again, and carried her back to the plush bed that we had been sleeping in every night since we had arrived here.

She lay down next to me, reached for my hand, and played with my fingers. I loved it when she touched me like that, so casual, as though she was still getting used to the thrill of having me right there, where she wanted me.

"How are you feeling?" I asked her as she traced her finger over the ring that she had slipped onto my hand earlier in the day.

"I can't believe that we're really married," she admitted, shaking her head. "It's... it's crazy, don't you think?"

"I think it makes perfect sense," I replied. "I've always known you were going to be my wife."

"Oh, really?" She laughed. "Even when I chewed you out the first time we met?"

"Oh, yeah, there was no doubt about it," I replied. "Anyone who could speak to me like that was someone I wanted to have in my life, you know?"

"You're crazy," she told me fondly, turning over so she could face me properly.

"And you're crazier, for marrying me," I replied, smoothing her hair back from her face.

"Yeah, something like that," she agreed. Her hair was just starting to grow back now, though it was still far shorter than it was before she'd had to cut it all off. I wondered if she missed it, sometimes, but I didn't want to ask – it seemed unfair to remind her of everything that had come before, especially when we had come so far to forget it.

"You don't mind, do you?" I asked her. "How much we've had to give up, I mean."

She shook her head.

"Of course I don't."

"You don't mind not being Nadia?"

She shrugged.

"I think Nadia had a whole lot of issues," she replied. "I'm okay with leaving her behind, I think. And besides – this new version, she gets to be your wife. I think I can live with that."

I smiled. It was a relief to hear her talking that way about our new lives together. We had so much we still needed to figure out, so much we needed to put together, but as long as we were here, as long as the two of us were doing it together, we could pull it off.

"What about you?" she asked.

"What about me?"

"You left a lot behind, too."

She was referring, of course, to my family business. Since we came out here, I had shuttered up everything, closed it all down. The FBI had been in touch, and I had been able to broker a deal that allowed us to get out of the country and stay that way as long as we didn't cause them any more trouble. Even though I had been the one to take out Nikita, they seemed willing to overlook that for now as long as I was out of their hair. They didn't have to worry about the Salieris or the Serbians, and that must have come as a relief.

"I know," I replied. "But I was done with that part of my life. My father wanted me to get away from it, so I have."

She closed her eyes and yawned. She must have been exhausted. Even after being here for a good few weeks, it was hard not to let the strange time difference bother us. There was still a lot to get used to in these new lives that we were making for ourselves, but I was willing to put in the effort.

Especially now that we were married. We had a whole life ahead of us to work out the details. And, from this moment on, I intended to put all my energy into doing just that.

Epilogue – Nadia

"You want to grab some ice cream?" Andreas asked me, and I shook my head and yawned.

"Nah, I think I just want to get home," I replied, tucking my hand into his. "Is that okay?"

"More than okay," he replied, flashing me a smile. "You have no idea how much I've wanted to get you out of that dress all night…"

I laughed. The streets around us were bustling with people, the Gold Coast lit up for their summertime, but I felt like I might as well have been here alone with him. That's how it always felt, when we were together – it had been nearly two months since we had gotten married, but I still felt that same, sweet, dizzying delight of having him close to me that I had from the first moment I slipped the ring onto his finger.

But tonight – tonight felt different. We'd been out with some friends of ours, a few families my father had connected with since he had arrived, and now, we were heading back to our place. The air seemed still, like the whole city was holding its breath. But why? It was a night like any other. Nothing was going to happen. And yet…

"You okay?" he asked, and I nodded.

"Yeah, I'm fine," I replied. "Just tired. I haven't been around that many people at once in a while, you know?"

"Yeah, I feel you," he agreed, squeezing my hand and smiling. "But you were great. They were already talking about having us around again."

"Like my father would give us a choice," I laughed. He had put his roots down in this city quickly, made it his home; he had friends he went to the beach with every day, to work out and play football with, and he was settling in like he had been here his whole life. He wanted the same for us, too, though I was a little more reticent, a little more held-back. I supposed there was a part of me that worried about what people would think of us when they found out where we had come from.

"Yeah, point taken," he agreed as we turned the corner towards our house. We had moved out of the villa and into a little townhouse next to the beach, which we had turned into our sanctuary against the world. I always loved coming back here, knowing that we could hide away from everything with each other as long as we still had it.

But Andreas stopped dead in his tracks as soon as we laid eyes on the house. I furrowed my brow at him.

"Is everything okay?" I asked. He didn't reply. Slowly, he nodded towards the top story of the house.

"Do you see that?"

I followed his gaze, and my heart skipped several beats inside my chest as I realized what he was gesturing to. A light was on at the top of the building.

"Did you leave that on?" he asked, and I shook my head.

"I don't think so..."

"Shit," he muttered, and he strode towards the house. I tried to pull him back.

"Andreas, wait!" I pleaded with him. "Come on, be sensible – we can't just burst in there, what if someone's waiting for us—"

"They're not going to screw up everything that I have here," he growled, as he jammed the key into the lock and pushed the door open. I followed him, close behind, heart racing, all the fear that had seemed to drift away since we had come here flooding back to me in full force. What was happening? Who the hell was up there?

The house was still and quiet, but that didn't do much to reassure me. I needed to get him out of here. What if someone had found us? What if someone was here to take revenge against everything that we had done? Someone in Nikita's family, perhaps, determined to put this right?

He stormed up the stairs and I rushed up behind him. Did we have anything to protect ourselves, if something was going down? I had no idea. Andreas had promised to protect me, but I hadn't thought that he was going to have to.

He pushed open the bedroom door, and froze on the spot.

"What? What is it?" I called after him, fear lancing through me, taking control, all too familiar with the terror that was making it hard to breathe.

And when I rounded the corner and saw what he was looking at, I knew at once what had him so freaked out.

"Hello," Mauro announced as he stepped out of the bedroom, eyes darting between the two of us. "I suppose I owe the two of you a congratulations."

I stared at him. No way. No fucking way – there was just no way he could be here. He was dead. He had been for months. Andreas had told me, he had watched his body taken out of his apartment. And he had been wrecked over it, hurt, agonized over what he could have done to protect him better. And yet...

"Mauro?" Andreas breathed. Mauro nodded.

"The very same."

"You're dead."

"Not last time I checked."

I clung to Mauro as tight as I could. There wasn't any way this could be happening. Mauro was dead. And even if, by some strange twist of fate, he had survived everything that had happened... he was part of our old life. Part of the life we had left behind. We had moved on from all of this, and there wasn't a chance in hell that we were going to let anyone get in the way of that.

And yet, here he was, standing there before us like a ghost from our past. I wanted to blink and have him vanish, or shake myself awake next to Andreas in bed and tell him about the crazy dream I'd just had, but I couldn't.

Because this was real. As real as they came.

Another man stepped out from behind Mauro, and Andreas lurched back, covering me with his body – but he seemed to calm a little when he saw who it was.

"Leo," he muttered. The FBI guy? Another name I hadn't heard in a long time. I thought we had left that all behind, but maybe I should have known better than to believe it could really go like that. Our lives had been so wrapped around all of this for so long, but I had thought we had broken free.

Now I was being swiftly reminded that it wasn't so easy to get away from a past that you ached to leave behind.

"What are you doing here?" Andreas demanded. His voice was edged with tension, anger, confusion, everything I was feeling right now. I wished I could have console him. I was his wife, after all, I was meant to be able to help him with all of this, but in the face of the enormity of what was happening, I had no clue how I could.

"You need to come back," Mauro replied. The words that I had prayed I would never hear again, as long as we lived. I closed my eyes, trying to block it out, but that didn't do anything to shut out the reality of what was happening right in front of me.

Andreas tensed, shook his head.

"I'm not going anywhere," he growled.

"You have to," Mauro replied. "Back to New York. With us. That's why I'm here."

He tightened his grip on my hand, as though making sure I was still there with him. I squeezed it back, letting him know I hadn't gone anywhere.

"Why?"

"The Salieri family needs a leader," Mauro replied. Andreas shook his head.

"No, it doesn't," he replied, curtly. "It's over. I dissolved everything—"

"If you really think it's that easy," Mauro replied, picking his words carefully, narrowing his eyes at the two of us. "I'm not sure your father taught you anything."

I chewed my lip. I had feared this day would come. How long did we really have, before something like this was an inevitability? I should have known this would come back to find us, even though I wished I could hide from it. Even though I wished we could leave it behind us, for good.

"I have a life here, Mauro," Andreas replied, shaking his head. "You – I left everything behind in New York. I thought you were dead—"

"I needed to be, for a while," he answered calmly. How could he speak about it like it was nothing? Andreas had been sure that he had lost his friend, his closest confidante, and now Mauro was standing there as if he had just missed a call from him or something.

"But there's a power vacuum back there now," he explained. "We need someone to fill it. Someone we know we can trust. You're the only person we could agree on. So, we're here."

I could see the paleness in Andreas' face as he tried to come to terms with it. But he must have known it couldn't be that easy for him to abandon the life he had known. He must have guessed it would come back to find him one day, though he wished that it wouldn't. There was still so much we were trying to navigate, but we couldn't just leave behind everything that we had lived for in the past.

"You can't make us leave here."

"No, we can't," Mauro agreed. "But we can tell the Serbians where you're hiding and turn this place into a warzone in a matter of hours if you don't."

I shivered at the mere thought of it. Mauro and Leo might not have been ideal, but an assault from the Serbians would have been a million times worse.

Andreas closed his eyes. He knew he didn't have a choice – that we didn't have a choice. He turned to me, slowly, doubt written all over his face.

I was his wife. I was his wife, and that meant that I had agreed to help him through anything and everything that this world threw at him. No matter what they were asking him to do, I would do it right alongside him. It was the least I could do, to make sure he had someone supportive by his side, someone who would keep him on the right track, even when it felt like things were too impossibly difficult to imagine.

"Will you come with me?" he murmured. "If I go?"

I nodded at once.

"You know I will," I swore to him. "Anywhere you go, I go."

He paused.

"And do you think we can do this?"

"I know that you were always born to be a leader," I assured him. "You can do this. You can do anything. If this is what we need to do… we can do it."

I rolled back my shoulders, set my jaw. I meant it. Every word I said. No matter how much it scared me, we could survive anything this crazy world threw at us. When I held his hand, it was like everything else dropped away. The love between us was more than ever, stronger than it had ever been since I had worn his ring on my finger. We could do this, whatever they demanded of us, anything at all.

As long as we had each other.

Andreas turned back to Mauro, his hand still in mine, the two of us united against the world.

"I'll do it," he replied.

Mauro smiled.

"I thought you might," he replied. He glanced over to Leo, then clasped his hands together in front of him.

"Now," he replied. "I think we need to get out of here."

THE END

CLUB CONFESSION
urge
LEXY TIMMS
GET IT ON
Google Play
kobo
amazon
nook
Lexy Timms

Club Confession Series

Envy
Crave
Decoy
Urge
Path

Find Lexy Timms:

Lexy Timms Newsletter:
http://www.lexytimms.com/newsletter
Lexy Timms Facebook Page:
https://www.facebook.com/LexyTimmsAuthor
Lexy Timms Website:
http://www.lexytimms.com

Want

FREE READS?

Sign up for Lexy Timms' newsletter
And she'll send you updates on new releases,
ARC copies of books and a whole lotta fun!

S ign up for news and updates!
http://www.lexytimms.com/newsletter

More by Lexy Timms:

FROM BEST SELLING AUTHOR, Lexy Timms, comes a billionaire romance that'll make you swoon and fall in love all over again.

Jamie Connors has given up on men. Despite being smart, pretty, and just slightly overweight, she's a magnet for the kind of guys that don't stay around.

Her sister's wedding is at the foreground of the family's attention. Jamie would be fine with it if her sister wasn't pressuring her to lose weight so she'll fit in the maid of honor dress, her mother would get off her case and her ex-boyfriend wasn't about to become her brother-in-law.

Determined to step out on her own, she accepts a PA position from billionaire Alex Reid. The job includes an apartment on his property and gets her out of living in her parent's basement.

Jamie must balance her life and somehow figure out how to manage her billionaire boss, without falling in love with him.

** The Boss is book 1 in the Managing the Bosses series. All your questions won't be answered in the first book. It may end on a cliff hanger.

For mature audiences only. There are adult situations, but this is a love story, NOT erotica.

Faking It Description:

He groaned. This was torture. Being trapped in a room with a beautiful woman was just about every man's fantasy, but he had to remember that this was just pretend.

Allyson Smith has crushed on her boss for years, but never dared to make a move. When she finds herself without a date to her brother's upcoming wedding, Allyson tells her family one innocent white lie: that she's been dating her boss. Unfortunately, her boss discovers her lie, and insists on posing as her boyfriend to escort her to the wedding.

Playboy billionaire Dane Prescott always has a new heiress on his arm, but he can't get his assistant Allyson out of his head. He's fought his attraction to her, until he gets caught up in her scheme of a fake relationship.

One passionate weekend with the boss has Allyson Smith questioning everything she believes in. Falling for a wealthy playboy like Dane is against the rules, but if she's just faking it what's the harm?

A chance meeting with one of the company photographers may turn into more than just an impromptu photo shoot.

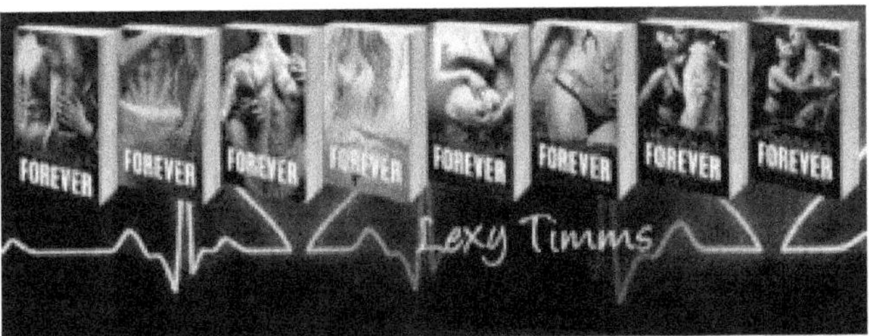

Book One is FREE!

Sometimes the heart needs a different kind of saving... find out if Charity Thompson will find a way of saving forever in this hospital setting Best-Selling Romance by Lexy Timms

Charity Thompson wants to save the world, one hospital at a time. Instead of finishing med school to become a doctor, she chooses a different path and raises money for hospitals – new wings, equipment, whatever they need. Except there is one hospital she would be happy to never set foot in again—her fathers. So of course, he hires her to create a gala for his sixty-fifth birthday. Charity can't say no. Now she is working in the one place she doesn't want to be. Except she's attracted to Dr. Elijah Bennet, the handsome heartbreaker chief.

Will she ever prove to her father that's she's more than a med school dropout? Or will her attraction to Elijah keep her from repairing the one thing she desperately wants to fix?

THE ONE YOU CAN'T FORGET

Emily Rose Dougherty is a good Catholic girl from mythical Walkerville, CT. She had somehow managed to get herself into a heap trouble with the law, all because an ex-boyfriend has decided to make things difficult.

Luke "Spade" Wade owns a Motorcycle repair shop and is the Road Captain for Hades' Spawn MC. He's shocked when he reads in the paper that his old high school flame has been arrested. She's always been the one he couldn't forget.

Will destiny let them find each other again? Or what happens in the past, best left for the history books?

** *This is book 1 of the Hades' Spawn MC Series. All your questions may not be answered in the first book.*

FORTUNE RIDERS INC
BILLIONAIRE BIKER
LEXY TIMMS
Download For
FREE
Lexy
Timms

ONE YOU CAN'T
forget
BESTSELLING AUTHOR
LEXY TIMMS
Lexy
Timms
Grab Your
FREE
Copy Today!

Bestselling Author
LEXY TIMMS
BEATING THE Biker

A BURNING LOVE SERIES

Book 1 – Spark of Passion
Book 2 – Flame of Desire
Book 3 – Blaze of Ecstasy

A Maybe Series

Book 1 – Maybe I Should

Book 2 – Maybe I Shouldn't

Book 3 – Maybe I Did

Don't miss out!

Visit the website below and you can sign up to receive emails whenever Lexy Timms publishes a new book. There's no charge and no obligation.

https://books2read.com/r/B-A-NNL-OCVXB

BOOKS 2 READ

Connecting independent readers to independent writers.

Did you love *Decoy*? Then you should read *Worth the Cost*[1] by Lexy Timms!

Some things are worth the cost of their consequences ...

Rosalee Clarkson isn't looking for love, she's looking for a temporary job.

When she landed the job working as Anthony Accardi's personal assistant, she could have never imagined things developing the way they had.

She was living in his guest house and getting full access to the man himself.

Things are explosive between them.

Sex with him is off the charts.

---

1. https://books2read.com/u/b5ryVl

2. https://books2read.com/u/b5ryVl

She knows it's wrong to sleep with the boss, but there is no denying the chemistry between them. When he asks her to go to Italy on a business trip, she is forced to decide between what she wants and what her heart demands.

Managing the Billionaire
Never Enough
Worth the Cost
Secret Admirers
Chasing Affection
Pressing Romance
Timeless Memories
Read more at www.lexytimms.com.

Also by Lexy Timms

12 Days of Christmas
Snowflake Hollow - Part 1
Snowflake Hollow - Part 2
Snowflake Hollow - Part 3
Snowflake Hollow - Part 4
Snowflake Hollow - Part 5
Snowflake Hollow - Part 6
Snowflake Hollow - Part 7
Snowflake Hollow - Part 8
Snowflake Hollow - Part 9
Snowflake Hollow - Part 10
Snowflake Hollow - Part 11
Snowflake Hollow - Part 12
Snowflake Hollow - Complete Series

A Bad Boy Bullied Romance
I Hate You
I Hate You A Little Bit
I Hate You A Little Bit More

A Bump in the Road Series
Expecting Love
Selfless Act
Doctor's Orders

A Burning Love Series
Spark of Passion
Flame of Desire
Blaze of Ecstasy

A Chance at Forever Series
Forever Perfect
Forever Desired
Forever Together

A Dark Casino Romance Series
High Roller
Place Your Bet
All Or Nothing

A Dark Mafia Romance Series
Taken By The Mob Boss
Truce With The Mob Boss
Taking Over the Mob Boss

Trouble For The Mob Boss
Tailored By The Mob Boss
Tricking the Mob Boss

A Dating App Series
I've Been Matched
You've Been Matched
We've Been Matched

A "Kind of" Billionaire
Taking a Risk
Safety in Numbers
Pretend You're Mine

A Maybe Series
Maybe I Should
Maybe I Shouldn't
Maybe I Did

A Royal Affair Series
Royally F*cked
Royally Screwed
Royally Obsessed

Assisting the Boss Series

Billion Reasons
Duke of Delegation
Late Night Meetings
Delegating Love
Suitors and Admirers

BBW Romance Series
Capturing Her Beauty
Pursuing Her Dreams
Tracing Her Curves

Beating the Biker Series
Making Her His
Making the Break
Making of Them

Betrayal at the Bay Series
Devil's Bay
Devil's Deceit
Devil's Duplicity

Billionaire Banker Series
Banking on Him
Price of Passion
Investing in Love
Knowing Your Worth

Treasured Forever
Banking on Christmas
Billionaire Banker Box Set Books #1-3

Billionaire CEO Brothers
Tempting the Player
Late Night Boardroom
Reviewing the Perfomance
Result of Passion
Directing the Next Move
Touching the Assets

Billionaire Hitman Series
The Hit
The Job
The Run

Billionaire Holiday Romance Series
Driving Home for Christmas
The Valentine Getaway
Cruising Love
Billionaire Holiday Romance Box Set

Billionaire in Disguise Series
Facade
Illusion

Charade

Billionaire Secrets Series
The Secret
Freedom
Courage
Trust
Impulse
Billionaire Secrets Box Set Books #1-3

Blind Sight Series
See Me
Fix Me
Eyes On Me

Branded Series
Money or Nothing
What People Say
Give and Take

Building Billions
Building Billions - Part 1
Building Billions - Part 2
Building Billions - Part 3

Butler & Heiress Series
To Serve
For Duty
No Chore
All Wrapped Up

Change of Heart Series
The Heart Needs
The Heart Wants
The Heart Knows

Club Confession Series
Envy
Crave
Decoy

Cottage by the Sea Series
Surging Tide
Distant Shores
Twisting Ocean

Counting the Billions
Counting the Days
Counting On You

Counting the Kisses

Cry Wolf Reverse Harem Series
Beautiful & Wild
Misunderstood
Never Tamed

Darkest Night Series
Savage
Vicious
Brutal
Sinful
Fierce

Diamond in the Rough Anthology
Billionaire Rock
Billionaire Rock - part 2

Dirty Little Taboo Series
Flirting Touch
Denying Pleasure
Forbidding Desire
Craving Passion

Dominating PA Series

Her Personal Assistant - Part 1
Her Personal Assistant - Part 2
Her Personal Assistant Box Set

Fake Billionaire Series
Faking It
Temporary CEO
Caught in the Act
Never Tell A Lie
Fake Christmas
Fake Billionaire Box Set #1-3

Firehouse Romance Series
Caught in Flames
Burning With Desire
Craving the Heat
Firehouse Romance Complete Collection

Forging Billions Series
Dirty Money
Petty Cash
Payment Required

For His Pleasure
Elizabeth
Georgia

Madison

Fortune Riders MC Series
Billionaire Biker
Billionaire Ransom
Billionaire Misery
Fortune Riders Box Set - Books #1-3

Fragile Series
Fragile Touch
Fragile Kiss
Fragile Love

Great Temptation Series
The Devil's Footsteps
Heaven's Command
Mortals Surrender

Hades' Spawn Motorcycle Club
One You Can't Forget
One That Got Away
One That Came Back
One You Never Leave
One Christmas Night
Hades' Spawn MC Complete Series

Hard Rocked Series
Rhyme
Harmony
Lyrics

Heart of Stone Series
The Protector
The Guardian
The Warrior

Heart of the Battle Series
Celtic Viking
Celtic Rune
Celtic Mann
Heart of the Battle Series Box Set

Heistdom Series
Master Thief
Goldmine
Diamond Heist
Smile For Me
Your Move
Green With Envy
Saving Money

Chasing Justice
Pursuing Justice
Justice - Complete Series

Karma Series
Walk Away
Make Him Pay
Perfect Revenge

King of Hades MC Series
Sinner
Tempting Sinner

Kissed by Billions
Kissed by Passion
Kissed by Desire
Kissed by Love

Leaning Towards Trouble
Trouble
Discord
Tenacity

Love on the Sea Series
Ships Ahoy

Rough Sea
High Tide

Lovers in London Series
Risking Millions
Venture Capital
Worth the Expense
The Price of Luxury
Exclusive Passion
Sparkling Christmas
Lovers in London - 3 Book Box Set

Love You Series
Love Life
Need Love
My Love

Managing the Billionaire
Never Enough
Worth the Cost
Secret Admirers
Chasing Affection
Pressing Romance
Timeless Memories
Managing the Billionaire Box Set Books #1-3

Managing the Bosses Series
The Boss
The Boss Too
Who's the Boss Now
Love the Boss
I Do the Boss
Wife to the Boss
Employed by the Boss
Brother to the Boss
Senior Advisor to the Boss
Forever the Boss
Christmas With the Boss
Billionaire in Control
Billionaire Makes Millions
Billionaire at Work
Precious Little Thing
Priceless Love
Valentine Love
The Cost of Freedom
Trick or Treat
The Night Before Christmas
Gift for the Boss - Novella 3.5
Managing the Bosses Box Set #1-3
Managing the Bosses Novellas

Mislead by the Bad Boy Series
Deceived
Provoked
Betrayed

Model Mayhem Series
Shameless
Modesty
Imperfection

Moment in Time
Highlander's Bride
Victorian Bride
Modern Day Bride
A Royal Bride
Forever the Bride

Mountain Millionaire Series
Close to the Ridge
Crossing the Bluff
Climbing the Mount

My Best Friend's Sister
Hometown Calling
A Perfect Moment
Thrown in Together

My Darker Side Series
Darkest Hour

Time to Stop
Against the Light

Neverending Dream Series
Neverending Dream - Part 1
Neverending Dream - Part 2
Neverending Dream - Part 3
Neverending Dream - Part 4
Neverending Dream - Part 5
Neverending Dream Box Set Books #1-3

Outside the Octagon
Submit
Fight
Knockout

Protecting Diana Series
Her Bodyguard
Her Defender
Her Champion
Her Protector
Her Forever
Protecting Diana Box Set Books #1-3

Protecting Layla Series
His Mission

His Objective
His Devotion

Racing Hearts Series
Rush
Pace
Fast

Regency Romance Series
The Duchess Scandal - Part 1
The Duchess Scandal - Part 2

Reverse Harem Series
Primals
Archaic
Unitary

Roommate Wanted Series
The Roommate
The Bunkmate
The Flatmate

R&S Rich and Single Series
Alex Reid
Parker

Sin Series
Payment for Sin
Atonement Within
Declaration of Love

Southern Romance Series
Little Love Affair
Siege of the Heart
Freedom Forever
Soldier's Fortune

Spanked Series
Passion
Playmate
Pleasure

Spelling Love Series
The Author
The Book Boyfriend
The Words of Love

Strength & Style
Suits You, Sir
Tailor Made

Perfect Gentleman

Taboo Wedding Series
He Loves Me Not
With This Ring
Happily Ever After

Tattooist Series
Confession of a Tattooist
Surrender of a Tattooist
Heart of a Tattooist
Hopes & Dreams of a Tattooist

Tennessee Romance
Whisky Lullaby
Whisky Melody
Whisky Harmony

The Bad Boy Alpha Club
Battle Lines - Part 1
Battle Lines

The Brush Of Love Series
Every Night
Every Day

Every Time
Every Way
Every Touch
The Brush of Love Series Box Set Books #1-3

The City of Mayhem Series
True Mayhem
Relentless Chaos
Broken Disorder

The Debt
The Debt: Part 1 - Damn Horse
The Debt: Complete Collection

The Fire Inside Series
Dare Me
Defy Me
Burn Me

The Gentleman's Club Series
Gambler
Player
Wager

The Golden Game

On The Pitch
Respect the Game
All Game
Sweat and Tears
The Final Score
The Golden Game Box Set Books #1-3

The Golden Mail
Hot Off the Press
Extra! Extra!
Read All About It
Stop the Press
Breaking News
This Just In
The Golden Mail Box Set Books #1-3

The Lucky Billionaire Series
Lucky Break
Streak of Luck
Lucky in Love

The Millionaire's Pretty Woman Series
Perfect Stranger
Captive Devotion
Sweet Temptations

The Sound of Breaking Hearts Series
Disruption
Destroy
Devoted

The University of Gatica Series
The Recruiting Trip
Faster
Higher
Stronger
Dominate
No Rush
University of Gatica - The Complete Series

Timing is Everything Series
Right Time
Right Place
Right Reasons

T.N.T. Series
Troubled Nate Thomas - Part 1
Troubled Nate Thomas - Part 2
Troubled Nate Thomas - Part 3

Toxic Touch Series
Noxious
Lethal
Willful
Tainted
Craved
Toxic Touch Box Set Books #1-3

Undercover Boss Series
Marketing
Finance
Legal

Undercover Series
Perfect For Me
Perfect For You
Perfect For Us

Unknown Identity Series
Unknown
Unpublished
Unexposed
Unsure
Unwritten
Unknown Identity Box Set: Books #1-3

Unlucky Series
Unlucky in Love
UnWanted
UnLoved Forever

War Torn Letters Series
My Sweetheart
My Darling
My Beloved

Wet & Wild Series
Stormy Love
Savage Love
Secure Love

Worth It Series
Worth Billions
Worth Every Cent
Worth More Than Money

You & Me - A Bad Boy Romance
Just Me
Touch Me
Kiss Me

Watch for more at www.lexytimms.com.

About the Author

"Love should be something that lasts forever, not is lost forever." Visit USA TODAY BESTSELLING AUTHOR, LEXY TIMMS https://www.facebook.com/SavingForever *Please feel free to connect with me and share your comments. I love connecting with my readers.* Sign up for news and updates and freebies - I like spoiling my readers! http://eepurl.com/9i0vD website: www.lexytimms.com Dealing in Antique Jewelry and hanging out with her awesome hubby and three kids, Lexy Timms loves writing in her free time. MANAGING THE BOSSES is a bestselling 10-part series dipping into the lives of Alex Reid and Jamie Connors. Can a secretary really fall for her billionaire boss?

Read more at www.lexytimms.com.

www.ingramcontent.com/pod-product-compliance
Lightning Source LLC
Chambersburg PA
CBHW061518120726
48001CB00004B/1352